# THE DAY I DIED

Thelonius D. Chestang

A JAPOC Industries Inc affiliated author

A.K.A. JAPOC

Just Another Piece of Clay

Isaiah 64:8

**Stay connected to me online and get on the mailing list at:
www.iamjapoc.com**

i

# JAPOC Industries Incorporated

ISBN: 978-1-7350887-0-9
Library of Congress Control Number: 2020939472

JAPOC Industries books are available at large quantities with special discounts for sales promotions, or for use in events. For more information, please contact a representative with JAPOC Industries Inc. by emailing JAPOC@cfl.rr.com or Info@iamjapoc.com.

First Printing: 2020
All scripture quotation, unless otherwise noted, are taken from the Holy Bible, King James Version or New International Version.

KJV – King James Version. Authorized King James Version 1973, 1978, 1984
NIV – Holy Bible, New International Version, 1973, 1978, 1984. Used by Permission.

For speaking engagements, please email JAPOC@cfl.rr.com
Author's website: www.iamjapoc.com

# THE DAY
# I DIED

# Disclaimers

The material in this book is for entertainment purposes only. The example of personal growth illustrated in this book is a dramatization and in no way should be taken as specific advice on how to handle real life situations. The author and publisher expressly disclaim any responsibility for any adverse effects resulting from applying any concepts or ideologies exemplified in this book. This work is a work of fiction. Therefore, names, characters, businesses, places, events, locales, and incidents are either the products of the author's imagination or used in a fictitious manner. Any resemblance to actual persons, living or dead, or actual events is purely coincidental.

This work also makes use infrequent, non-gratuitous use of profanity and violence solely for the purpose of adding realism to situational conflict. This work also highlights some difficulties in marriage which may resonate an intense emotional response from the reader. While the author has taken great length to ensure the subject matter is dealt with in a compassionate and respectful manner, it maybe troubling for some readers. Discretion is advised.

# Reviews

*Could not put it down and read it in one sitting! We meet the main character shortly after he has a vision/premonition of his own death occurring in the next 24 hours. Through the rest of the story we are taken along on his journey as he checks off the items on his list he feels he needs to do/resolve before his time is up. I found myself cheering him on as he goes through his journey and found it interesting the impact these deeds have on him as well as others. Hope you enjoy it as much as I did.*
—Jeff Togie, Minister

*The premise of the story is strong. It is not cliché at all. I felt pulled into Johnny's life. I was pulling for him, worrying about him, cheering for him. That is what you want your readers to do. The ending was gripping. The scene at the church with the news cameras was powerful.*
*Then... I read your poem. Wow! Life-changing. This is a groundbreaking, earth-shaking truth.*
— Angela Costa, Freelance Editor, Fiver.com

*The Day I Died is a compelling story with an ending that I didn't see coming, but made perfect sense. A supernatural thriller dressed in ordinary circumstances. I read it in one sitting, but the profound messages of redemption and rebirth reverberated long after I finished. Highly recommended!*
— Poinciana Willis

*Uplifting and thought-provoking story. We follow Johnny Box (John Boxton), the main character, through a day he believes to be his last on earth. Along the way we get the opportunity to see his good points and his flaws - and recognize that he is as human as we are. His faith in God is clear as he moves through his checklist of tasks he wants to complete before he dies. Very enjoyable read.*
— Deborah Schaffer

# Dedication

To my wife, Angela Chestang, who is the steady light on my journey often shrouded in uncertainty. To my daughter Devyn, whose chronic medical conditions have not stopped her from knowing joy, showing joy and giving me joy. To my son, Donovan, who has learned so many things so much sooner than I did, I love you and I pray you find your path to peace and to your highest contribution to this world.

# Acknowledgements

I want to acknowledge my friends and family for their support in my drive to more fully embrace the path of a writer which I have only just recently embarked upon.

Thank you to my friend and cousin, Larry Roundtree II, for his support and for inspiring this work.

To my friend and mentor, Anderson Hill II, thank you for your encouragement always.

To my cousin, Rick, thanks for always being a help to me in my journey as a writer.

To my friends and former colleagues Deborah Schaffer and Sandra Wagner. Thank you for agreeing to be early reviewers and providing your inputs and suggestions.

To Pastor J. Roy Morrison, thank you for opening the path for Mount Pleasant Church to support my work.

To my sister Poinciana and to Carey, thanks for always being there to support my attempts to promote my works.

To my father, thank you for always being the first or second person to read my books. To my mother, thank you for all your prayers in support of my journey.

To my friend Jeff Togie, thank you for your friendship and for being a fan of my work.

To my friend Eddie Coleman, you are the most like-minded person on the earth to me. I value having your input to help me think through some of my most challenging moments as an entrepreneur and a spiritualist.

To my friend Greg Abellard, your entrepreneurial drive and creativity have helped me to stay on track and embrace this journey perhaps more than anyone. You have taught me to "Trust the Process."

To my wife Angie, thank you for supporting a journey that is foreign to you despite all the uncertainty I have asked to you endure.

# Table of Contents

# Prologue

I started writing this book in 2010. It came to an abrupt halt as I, honestly, had nothing more than a mental flash of what the book should be. It wasn't until my cousin, Larry Roundtree II, invited me to his church to hear him speak about his own journey that things began to click. I had decided in the spring of 2018 that my writing was going to have a message—the message of JAPOC. But what was the essence of that message going to be? It needed to be something people could understand and utilize.

I realized that my second and third works, the Forbidden Fruit volumes, were really an allegory, or perhaps a modern-day parable. After hearing a bit of my cousin's story, I knew I wanted to wrap this message of JAPOC into a preacher's journey. It was amazing to have an entire book unfold in my mind at once. The stories of Jonah and my cousin blended and plunged deep into my imagination.

At the same time, in my own journey, I was experiencing a sense of freedom that evolved after committing to exploring my own authenticity as well as my identity as a writer. I experienced a moment of profound freedom in my mind and spirit which I have described my poem below: Real Freedom. I have been guilty of attaching freedom to my unobtained material goals or my measured milestones. But I also see that there are many that have already achieved some of the things I pursue, yet happiness or fulfillment still seem to elude them. I have decided that if freedom is contingent upon achieving things that can be taken away, then that is not freedom at all. In my moment of profound freeness, my heart was full of gratitude for all that I had achieved and those in my life that love me and helped me to achieve them. My heart was filled with a desire to give and to express that gratitude in my service to the world. It is more blessed to give than to receive

(Acts 20:35). When I felt that in my heart, I felt an overwhelming sense of liberty that I wanted to share with the world.

I was able to free myself of my own regrets and disappointments. I was also able to disconnect my sense of value and peace from the things that I still strive to achieve. I am still a very goal-oriented, ambitious person, but I will not think less of myself nor will I allow myself to become discontent if I do not achieve my goals. My sense of freedom is not contingent upon any of these things. I now realize that I have been on a path towards this sense of freedom for many years; when I wrote Magnificent Me in 2010 and These Things in 2015 (see www.iamjapoc.com poems) I was evolving towards this point of view.

When I wrote, Forbidden Fruit, I was attempting to propose the question, "What's in it for me to worship God?" I gave an example of a life of a person that had all of life's material problems figured out – or so he thought. Toward the end of the book, the main character realizes that a sense of purpose was more valuable than the resources used to pursue any particular purpose. In this book, I attempt to answer the same question with an additional answer; profound peace - freedom.

As the Stoic philosophers would say, Freedom is a choice and it is a one you can make today. This is also the message of Jesus Christ which is an opposite view of reality from the world. If you have more faith in the Creat-OR than the Creat-ED, you too can also know this freedom.

This freedom also gives you the capacity to do something you can feel good about today. If your life were going to end before morning tomorrow, what would you do with the time you have left?

# Real Freedom

A Poem by Thelonius D. Chestang

I had a moment of clarity, an awakening of a kind.
I felt freedom within my heart. I felt freedom in my mind.

I felt fully unencumbered from any particular thing of want.
As if a ruddy, ghost filled building, became no place to haunt.

An epiphany of sudden freeness, for the taking all this time.
These worldly things of cost which have no value, not a dime

Things of greatest value are not purchased but must be earned.
Character, trust, confidence and all the things that we might learn.

The carnal mind will never know this, to which this cannot be
explained.
Pursuit of a thing has value though the thing itself be abstained

In order to gain independence - The stoics might have said.
Knowledge of what you are reading is worth less than to say you
read.

The path you bled fiercely upon pursuing the hard-earned prize
Was filled with greater truth than the shiny bundle of lies.

I wish to encourage you, my reader to fully embrace your path.
Though it promises no glory and yet is filled with wrath.

I encourage you to find that stillness that speaks only to your heart.
That you would pause your ceaseless worry, there is no better
start.

My own heart filled with peace having no room for carnal need.
gave way to deeper yearning, to plant a kind of seed.

I pray for unknown harvest, a bounty of unknown fruit.
Which blesses my neighbor and my family; by message I must root.

And share a sense of gratitude for you, my brother and my friend.
As if a true and spiritual energy became a currency I now spend.

Still tied to financial agreements which lay claim upon my life
But with an ethereal freedom from all related strife.

I feel freedom in my heart, freedom in my mind.
Freedom in my spirit though I yet pursue the grind.

With no need of worldly gains or any specific thing to receive
I have only a dire need of giving, sharing things that I believe

To give that which flows within me, it leaves no room for shallow
things
I reject all of the disillusionment achievement often brings.

I yet quest to accomplish more. To learn and grow in things I
choose.
But I quest to receive no thing. Therefore, there is no thing to lose.

We may choose a spirit of fullness or we may choose one drawn to
drought
There is a duty to your own becoming. I pray we all would seek it
out.

I pray my own understanding would continue without pause.
That my peace grow ever deeper and that the world would know
my cause.

# One Hell of a Day

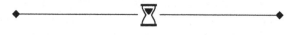

My name is John. My last name ...well, it doesn't even matter. I won't be alive tomorrow. I haven't done a single thing in my life that will last beyond a week. I don't have any kids...anymore. I'm not married...not anymore...I don't think. My friends are a collection of people that I owe and who would rather not see me coming. I have one brother...he's really my cousin. He loves me and he's worse off than me. He's the one person in the world that might miss me. My dad already wrote me off...I think.

I have known clearly in my heart that God chose me to be a preacher. I couldn't even go to church and sit quietly in the pews without seeing things I didn't want to see...like flashes of a future I did not want responsibility for. My father is a preacher and I saw enough to know I could not live up to that standard. I don't guess there's any point praying about it. I have known that this is what I was on this planet to do for many years. I guess you can only say No to God for so long; forty-two years of nothing coming to a sudden end.

I awoke in a puddle lying in my bed. It was a big puddle. I swished in the water sitting up, looking at the ceiling to see if the water had come from it. The ceiling was dry and I didn't have a roommate to plan such a prank on me. My dream was still crisp in my mind. A hero, from comic book I used to read, was about to drown me. The words on his lips said, "Today, you die" as his beastly hands pushed me under.

I awoke suddenly from the dream and either I had just died or was about to die. I knew this as plainly as I now sat in this puddle of water. I was soaked from my head to my toe. I stood and looked down at the puddle, wiping water from my face and squeezing it out of my hair. "It's not real," I said.

A loud voice boomed in my head in a loud kind of silence, "Make peace." The words were clear like a terrifying shout in my mind.  My body recoiled as I closed my eyes and I saw a large, shining hourglass in the dark. The puddle was real. And with the image of the hourglass, I knew I would die before the end of the day. I wasn't sure what make peace meant. But I knew someplace deep in my spirit that God was telling me to get ready for my own end.  My time was already running out.

I looked around my smelly, studio apartment. I lived in a rat hole above a rat's nest. The rat's nest was full of cars I couldn't afford. I loved cars; both finished and those in need of work.  I never saw a car that I hated. But right now, I hate my apartment.  I hated the way it looked, smelled and made me feel – like, I was better than this.  So, I started cleaning it. I found a few dollars but mostly cleaning helped me clear my head. I still knew I was gonna die today.  I felt it like a dull sickness in my belly that I could scarcely ignore. Even more specifically, I somehow knew my death would involve water.  It was eerie to have such a specific impression about your own impending death. Mostly, though, I wanted to force myself to think about how I wanted to go out. I want to go out on some sort of high note, like a hall-of-fame athlete having a monstrous game on the day he announced his retirement. I'd like to go out like a hero. Yeah, it would be nice to die saving somebody. I could get a memorial or something.

I caught my reflection in a cheap framed mirror over a bureau in the eating area. It was a look of sincere satisfaction. *Yes, if today is my day to die, I'll die a hero... if I can.*

I eventually finished cleaning. My place looked even cleaner than it looked when I moved in. I had bags and bags of stuff I was keeping but I didn't really need: magazines, newspapers, decks of cards missing cards. I had an old combination printer/fax machine that didn't print and probably didn't fax. I had cheap plastic plants that had thin layers of dust on all the leaves. I had a bulletin board with all sorts of stuff stuck on it, dreams about things I'd eventually do. I wouldn't get to do any of those things. Nope. No bucket list for me. No fancy homes with lavish enclosed pools. No fancy cars. I wrote a check to myself for ten million dollars postmarked for three years from next month. I almost tore it up months ago. Something made me hold onto it. I decided to fold it up and put it in my pocket. *Yeah. I'll die a rich man*, I laughed to myself.

I took the last of the bags I filled with stuff I wasn't going to need anymore and took it downstairs to the trash pile. I tossed it up, but the bag fell short of the opening of the dumpster and half of it hung inside the dumpster and the other half hung outside. I hadn't tied the top, just pulled the drawstring, so the stuff I'd put in the bag was scattered across the asphalt in front of the dumpster opening. I knelt to pick up the trash and one magazine had words on the cover that hit my mind kinda hard.

"MAKE PEACE ..." I ignored the rest of the words. It was an old Time magazine reflecting past days and conflicts about wars. Make Peace? How am I supposed to do that? Go to Washington D.C. today and make a big presentation to Congress? I tossed the magazine and the rest of the trash into the dumpster. As I reached the top of the stairs, I heard a phone ringing. It was mine. I extended my strides and entered the open door of my upstairs apartment. I'd left my phone in the kitchen. The caller ID showed "Duck." I answered it.

"Duck! What's up, man?" I was glad to hear from my cousin.

Duck seemed to be gathering his words, "Yo, cuz. I'm in a bad spot man."

"What you need, man?" I asked.

"That $300 you owe me. If I don't get it today, I'm in trouble man...with Erick," Duck explained.

Duck was once a high-profile football player. He was a wide receiver, fast, nimble, and crafty...until he messed up a knee in college. He tried rehab without surgery and only made it worse when he tried to return. Then he had to have a surgery he couldn't afford, and he got cut from the team. He returned home in disgrace to very little opportunity. He got a factory job and got hurt there, too. The company fired him for not following safety procedures—procedures that were neither practiced nor encouraged. But they were well posted, and he didn't follow them. The result, a busted vertebrae and regular pain that was only helped by smoking marijuana or popping some sort of illegal or heavily regulated pill he couldn't afford. Duck had resorted to getting either marijuana or medication from wherever he could whether he had money or not. I could guess what sort of trouble he was in. But today, he was in luck. I didn't have $300 but I did have things worth $300 that I was willing to sell. I wouldn't be around to use them after today anyway.

"I thought Erick was gonna be your manager way back...before you started with that other guy. How did he become your dealer?" I was confused.
"He ain't the kid you remember from the sports highlights, man. He was in music outta nowhere. Then, his dad went to jail and then he got outta music. Next thing I knew he had products. I don't know the whole story." Duck became silent.
I don't got it, Duck ...but I'll get it. I'll get it to you today, man."
"Thank you, Johnny. Thank you. I'll be home."

So, now I knew what *Make Peace* meant. It meant paying my debts. Paying what I owe. The words were clear. Make your peace. Since I know today is my day, I guess it's pretty cool that I have a chance to go out clean, not like a piece of trash guy that everyone probably is glad to see gone. Ok. That's it then. I will die debt-free. That's how I'll make my peace. It would really be cool if I could die a hero...like, save somebody's life. I mean, I could have a bridge or a street or something named after me. I paused for a moment. Yeah, that's how I will die. None of this crap matters really. It's the last things you do that matter. The last things I do will be pretty freaking spectacular!
I felt oddly grateful ...knowing that today was going to be my day and having a chance to decide how I use it. It occurred

to me that really...I had that opportunity all of my life. We all do. But right now, I WILL do great things with the time I have left. If today's my day to die, I'm goin' out in sparkling fashion. I found a Superhero t-shirt that needed to be put away. I decided to put it on. Today's gonna be one hell of a day.

# The List

I finished cleaning and sat down to make a list of things and people I owed debts to. I leaned back into my old, ragged couch. The faces of all the people I knew or could remember flashed across my mind like pages of a book as I flicked a pen back and forth in my fingers. Sometimes I paused on certain faces checking my heart to see if I felt completely at peace that I owed them nothing. But every now and then I paused on a face and couldn't move on. Those names I wrote down.

Some people I owed money to. Others I had held onto items belonging to them that I, for no particular reason other than laziness, never returned them. I had a leather jacket somewhere in my apartment that wasn't mine.

There was also the thing about collections. I had a collection of toy cars, still in the box. I liked to collect other things, but I only had a couple of real collections. I loved cars, but I was working on real cars. Restoring cars for money while fantasizing about toy cars didn't really excite me as much now.

My wife's...ex-wife's...nephew Lilliard loved my toy car collection. Maybe I wanted him to have it before I died. If I gave it to him myself, I'd get to see the expression on his face. He was a very animated guy, which is likely why he was such a successful sales guy. He worked for an IT company downtown and he didn't travel much anymore since he went into management. He might actually be around for me to give him that box of unopened model cars. Yeah, the thought that they went to someone who admired them more than me made me feel good. I added his name and the box of cars to the list.

I ended the list. It was shorter than I thought it should be. It seemed like there were names missing, but I couldn't really be sure who needed to be added. It seemed right to add my wife's...ex-wife's...name, but I couldn't say for what exactly. Should I apologize to her for being who I am or was...that didn't seem like enough, but what more should I say? Do I even agree that I have anything to apologize for?

My stomach did strange things at the thought I was going to die today. I didn't want to think about death. I wanted to think about life. I wanted to think about the good I did. I wanted to remember my life today and feel excited about something that I would know people would remember. I wanted to be remembered for something good.

But what about people who don't do good; what happens to them? I suddenly remembered a man that bullied me – whom I allowed to bully me. He bullied me physically when I was young. Later, I got trained and had skills to fight. Then, he bullied me with his words, and I did nothing. He was a big man but, in this moment, I bet that I could have taken him. I never tried – instead, I let him bully me in High School. I don't owe him anything, but I thought about him in my list. I wasn't sure what to do about this particular memory, so I put my list down.

I got up and found a shirt to wear on top of my superhero t-shirt. I wanted to look nice on my last day alive and my first day becoming a hero. I took a little time to iron some pants and a very nice shirt I got from a thrift store. Someone who had more money than time donated a fancy name brand shirt, and it was just my size.

BANG – BANG, someone was knocking on the door to my apartment with a heavy hand. BANG – BANG.

"What?!" I blurted out in anger at the person who was spoiling my moment.

"Come down to the garage." It was Jim.

Jim owned the building and the garage/storage space downstairs. He rented space for cars and boats and let me use part of his shop to restore cars. I also worked for him. He would get cars from people I was never supposed to see to fix cars that had been places they should never have been. I didn't ask questions I didn't want to know answers to. It was a slow business, but when he got a call, I had to drop whatever I was doing to make a car look like brand new. Jim allowed me to stay in the room upstairs in exchange for fixing whatever he brought to me. I also didn't have to pay for the space I used to restore cars for my customers, which was also a slow business. Money was thin and came sporadically, but whatever money I made restoring cars was mostly mine...minus helping Jim with utilities. I also supported Jim's alcohol habit by buying him drinks and regulating how much he drank. That was my life...our life, Jim and me. We fixed cars, we drank, we talked about cars. He talked about women, and I thought about my wife...ex-wife.

"Hey, Jim, come here for a minute," I called out to him.

"What?" he grunted from beyond the door to my apartment.

"Just come here!" I demanded. I heard his footfalls getting closer. The door opened.

"What?" he grunted again.

"Do you see this?" I asked pointing to the bed in my studio apartment still full of water. Jim walked over to the bed and stared at it for a moment. Then he looked at me suspiciously.

"Do you see the water?" I asked. Jim looked at me again as though I were up to something. I shrugged my shoulders.

Jim looked at the ceiling and then scanned the room. He grunted a bit more before getting down on one knee. He searched under the bed for several seconds. He got up on a knee and pulled his cell phone out of his pocket. He switched on the light and returned to inspecting the underside of the bed.

He stood with a curious look on his face. He put his hand in the water, rubbed his wet fingers together, gave them a sniff, and dried his hands on his pants.

He smiled at me, "You're good." He turned to leave my apartment. "You're good," he said walking out. I was expecting some sort of an explanation—not an accusation.

"That's not me!" I insisted. "I don't know how that happened."

Jim didn't stop his stride. "When you're done with your bullshit, I'll be in the garage," Jim chided me. He'd dismissed the entire event. I knew he'd give it no further thought. I was left alone with the miracle of this morning as well as the message—Make Peace. I was alone to face my fate.

The sick feeling in my stomach intensified. I took a deep breath and remembered that, although I may not be able to decide how my day will end, I would do everything I can until that moment comes to make my best use of what time I have left.

I eventually caught up to Jim downstairs in the garage. The floor squeaked under my shoes. He kept the floor clean, a ritual that Jim seemed to take pride in. He demanded that his shop be kept clean or that I at least did not take away from whatever he did to keep it clean and organized. Jim's shop was his house and his church.

"Where's the starter?" I asked, immediately seeing that a part I ordered for my 1970 AMC Rebel Machine was gone.

It was a muscle car, and I loved the idea of what it was going to look and sound like when it was done. It was a shell, nothing but potential. I spent the last five years finding and ordering and sending back and reordering vintage parts. I was nearly done restoring the engine and close to done with the body. The body only needed painting. The engine only needed the right starter. The one I had left on the workshop table was the wrong part. It wasn't vintage, and I planned to mail it back.

"Did you do something with the starter, Jim? I gotta send that back."

Jim nodded his head. "Forget that. I got sick of seeing it just sittin' there. You been working on that hot rod for years, and you're gon' let a technicality stop you from hearing it run?" Jim argued.

I took a deep breath. I was nervous. That might be the real reason that I hadn't put it in. It was the hardest car I ever worked on, and it was the only one that truly mattered to me. I wanted to make sure that only vintage parts were used, or it would take away from the value of the car. I had won the car in a silly bet when it was nothing more than a dusty heap of headache, maybe worth about $600. Whenever I finish painting it...well, if I had time to finish painting it...it would be worth about $60,000...but only if I used vintage parts. I never planned to sell it.

"Keys are in the ignition. I didn't have the heart to start it up. I know how hard you worked on it," Jim explained.
"What? You put that junk in my car?" I exclaimed.
"Hell yeah, I did!" Jim retorted. "Start the damn car. Let's hear it." Jim walked around to the passenger side and got in. "You did real nice work on this, Box. Looks good inside. Smells right. Let's see if them 340 horses sound right. Oh, I put you some 93-octane in there."

I exhaled shaking my head in anxiety and irritation. Well, today is my last day. I want to hear it too. I slid into the crisp leather seats.

"I'm still pissed at you for putting that crap on my car," I reminded Jim.
"Get over yer'self. Turn that key," Jim demanded, leaning his head back waiting for the sound.

I turned the ignition half hoping it wouldn't start and half excited to hear it. The engine coughed a bit at first, and then it turned over. After that, it purred. It absolutely purred. I gave it some gas, listening to the powerful engine. I looked over at Jim. His eyes were closed as he took in the sound of the engine respond to me giving it gas.

Finally, Jim looked over at me, "You did real good kid, real good." He buckled his seat belt and handed me one of the remotes to the garage door.

I pushed the button and the light began to pour into the garage and shone on my Rebel Machine for the first time in years.

I buckled my seat belt and took the car out slowly. I pulled away from the garage around from the back of the building to the street. I looked at Jim feeling very satisfied.
He smiled back at me and nodded. He didn't need to say anything.

I eased out onto the highway leading away from Jim's garage toward the outer part of the city. The car sounded great. I gave it more gas, and it quickly responded. When Jim rolled his window down, I knew that meant it was time to fly. I soon found an old country road further south away from civilization, and I gave it a good push. The car responded just as it would have in the 1970s. It felt nice to drive, and the breeze coming into the car only accentuated the feeling of freedom. I was glad to have felt this before I died today.

I drove back to the garage and pulled into the bay where it had sat for nearly the entire five years I owned it. I killed the ignition, and I felt awful. I remembered someone else's name and another thing I needed to add to the list.

"What's what kid?" Jim asked.
I rubbed my forehead. "This car isn't mine."
"What the hell you mean kid?"
"I cheated."
"Cheated? At what?" Jim asked
"A guy...Ricky, a guy that used to make bad bets. He was drunk, and we were playing poker. He had a straight. I had a flush...only I didn't have a flush. I stashed a card from an earlier

hand – I don't know why. Then when he had a straight, I already had the card I needed to win that hand. It was perfect, so...I cheated."

"What ya gonna do, kid?"

I took a deep breath. "Give it back... today."

Jim nodded. "Hell of a thing to do, kid. Hell of a thing." He got out of the car and walked away.

I went upstairs and added Ricky's name and the car to my list. I found the box of toy cars. I signed some papers and grabbed the leather jacket and a pair of M1905 Bayonets from World War II that I got from my grandfather. Together, they were worth about $1200, but I didn't have time to sell them for that price. I had been given an offer on them a few years back when I wanted to check the value. Maybe I could sell them today and start to pay off some debts.

I loaded up all the things I needed for today and walked to the door. I took a long look at my apartment, my home for the past year and a half. I went downstairs and loaded the items for the day into the back seat. I waved goodbye to Jim who didn't seem to notice. I didn't want to make a big deal even though I thought it was. Jim was a good man who made money doing good things for people who didn't seem very good at all.

I would be free of all of it now. Jim would never see me again, and I didn't know how to explain it to him. I didn't try. I slipped into my AMC Machine and took the car out of the garage. After the car was fully out of the garage, I got out, reached inside the opening, and hit the button on the wall. The door came down, and I watched it close. Good-bye Jim, I mumbled. I stared down at my list. Time to be a hero.

# Good-bye

I collected $650 from the pawnshop guy for my granddaddy's bayonets. Added to the rest of the money I had in the world, I now had $677.27. The car was pure joy to drive even at slower speeds. My attention to detail and pursuit of perfection was plain to see. This car was something to be proud of even unfinished. I felt great about it, and that seemed to give me an edge. That edge came in handy with Victor, the sleazy pawn shop guy. I heard stories about things he did to women who took things into his shop, and I hated having to deal with him. But he was the only shop I'd visited that wanted the bayonets. Besides, today Victor was somehow generous...if you could use that adjective with pawnshop guys.

I owed my cousin $300. I calculated my debts to Debbie to be about $230 in sympathy meals at her diner. I knew Debbie from high school...knew her – knew her. She still had sort of a crush on me. Today, I felt like I had been taking advantage of that all these years. But I also wanted to eat, and she could really cook.

I pulled into the diner's parking lot. A few guys standing in the hardware store parking lot next door knew enough about cars to be impressed with mine.

"Hey fella, is that a Machine?" an older man asked. He could have passed for Jim's older brother.

"1970," I answered.

"When you finish the bodywork, bring it by. I might take it off your hands," he teased.

I think he was teasing. It didn't matter. The car would never be his. It would only be mine for a little while longer. I smiled politely and turned toward the diner's entrance.

I opened the door of the diner, stirring the bell attached to the door handle. Debbie was standing near a table holding a half-full coffee pot. She smiled as I stepped into the building.

"Well...look at you," she said somehow joining me in my triumphant morning.

"Good morning Debbie. How ya been?"

"I am doing just fine and better now that I see you all cleaned up." She was almost grinning with pride.

"I wanted to say thank you for all the free meals and encouragement over the years while things weren't going so well for me...or maybe I just wasn't doing well for myself."

"So, I take it those days are over?" Debbie asked. She couldn't have known the accuracy of her words.

"Those days are over Debbie ...and I want to start my day with some of your cooking...if that's ok with you."

She was absolutely beaming now. Debbie was a spunky red head whose skin managed to tolerate some bit of a tan. She managed to stay slender all these years despite three children and a job working with food. She was always busy and bounced around her diner like a hummingbird.

Her hair was fire red to match her lipstick. The wrinkles around her mouth and eyes couldn't hope to diffuse her bright, cheery smile. I wanted a hug and she seemed to know it.

"Come on over here, old friend. Give a girl a hug, and then I'll sit you down and see about that empty belly o' yours. Debbie gave me a strong hug like you'd get with an aunt that loved you.

"Now, grab a table, man." As I sat, Debbie filled a coffee cup and set it in front of me.

"You having the regular today or XXXinningXXXg' special?"
I grinned.

"Today...I think will be one heck of a day, Debbie. Fill me up right."

She nodded slowly, "Well, alright then. House special ...kicked up a notch."

She bounced behind the counter, giving orders to one of her two cooks. She had much more to say to him than normal. She seemed to be explaining something he'd never heard before. At first, the cook looked puzzled. As she continued, he nodded a couple of times and then she turned to smile at me. I don't know what "kicked up a notch" meant, but I was expecting a glorious meal.

Debbie came to sit with me. "So...tell me all about it," she said still beaming.
"Well, I figure I owe you about two-hundred forty for all the meals."
"Two times a week, fifteen weeks, seven-dollar meals is two hundred ten. Thirty dollars for tips would be just fine," she said looking at me through her radiant smile as though the money was no longer an issue despite her calculations.
"Well add that to my bill for today," I explained. Debbie studied me for a moment. "It is really good to see you Johnny Box." She studied me further. "What are you up to?"

I wasn't sure exactly how to answer, so I thought about it. "Guess I just got tired of being the old me. Today ...today is about the new me...the me I oughtta be." That was the best I could come up with.
Debbie folded her fingers together still examining me and pondering my words. "Well..." she took a breath before finishing. "I hope today is all you hope for it to be." She slid out of the booth bench and stood beside me. Leaning toward me with her knee on my bench, she took my face in one of her hands and kissed me on the cheek. She stepped back and returned to the counter to check on my food and probably some other folks' meals.

There was another young waitress in the diner working on the other end now standing beside her collecting plates from the counter. She put a plate of bacon, eggs, and toast down in front of a nervous-looking young man. It seemed he had been looking at me, but he sharply turned away as I made eye contact.

Debbie spoke briefly to the young girl giving some instructions and the girl stacked the plates up her arm and returned to her end of the diner to distribute the food. Debbie turned me. Her furrowed brow told me she was contemplating something. I returned to my coffee and my own thoughts.

It wasn't long before Debbie returned to my booth with a set of plates lined up outstretched her arm with different kinds of food. My fork immediately went to the French toast, which I loved more than another other breakfast food. There was a thin steak covered in gravy, eggs with colorful vegetables in them, diced potatoes, and a small bowl of fruit.

She made a second trip now brandishing a cup of orange juice. I hadn't ordered French toast, but I guess Debbie remembered that I loved her French toast from high school so many years ago. She poured herself a cup of coffee and sat down across from me.

"You're eatin' with me or just sitting?" I asked. Debbie smiled, "I already ate." She sipped her coffee. "How's your daddy? Did he ever go back to preaching?"

"He did, "I answered. "After he took a year off and traveled. But we haven't spoken since..."

Tears formed in my eyes. It was a wound I had forgotten but was never healed of. Debbie patted my hands as I regained my composure and blinked tears back to wherever they were trying to come from.

She took another sip of her coffee. "I thought sure you'd be preaching by now. I expected to be sittin' in the pews of your church." She grinned. "All that XXXinning' we used to do...but, you still wanted to read that good book. Never saw anybody WANT to read it. I know your daddy made you read it, but I was...almost jealous. You used to love that bible, Johnny."

She took a sip of her coffee before continuing, "Is that what today is about?"

I knew my time was over, but Debbie was always very perceptive. Today she was wrong though. "Sorta...but...not really Deb." I looked out the window. "It's hard to explain." So I didn't.

"Well, I hope you figure it out. Feels like you come to say good-bye to me, Johnny Box." She nodded. "I'm real glad you stopped by first."

I slid out of the seat. I don't know why, but I wanted to kiss her. I stood taking her hands, pulling her closer to me. I kissed her. Every part of me just wanted her to know that I was grateful for her being in my life. She was a friend...a good friend.

Now staring in each other's eyes, Debbie teared up. "I been waiting for that kiss for a long time, Johnny Box." She patted on my chest, "And now I know for sure you came to say good-bye." She pulled away from me and headed toward the kitchen wiping her eyes.

I returned to my food. It was an outstanding last meal. The other waitress came to give me my bill. The bill was for two hundred forty. A little note read, "Meal today paid for with a kiss." The young waitress went back to her other customers. I counted out the $240 dollars and put it under one of my plates. I finished my coffee and slid out of the booth.

I had $437.27 to my name now. Three hundred of that was owed to my cousin, and I would see him next. The rest I could give to some church someplace or a homeless person. I wiped the leather jacket I was still borrowing. I had taken a last sip of the coffee and spilled some on it. Debbie didn't come out to say good-bye to me. I understood.

I was stuffed and there was still more food on my plate. I tried to eat most of everything, but I could only finish the French toast. I picked up a piece of pineapple and threw it into my mouth wondering what the day would bring.

I must have gotten lost in the moment because I turned to leave to find the nervous-looking young man standing in front of me with a small gun.

"Gimme that jacket and that wad o' cash old man.

It seemed like a joke. The young man took hold of my jacket at my chest and yelled out, "Everybody give me your money, or I kill this old man." He slid around behind me pointing the gun now at Debbie who was standing behind the counter. "I...I...I want the money from the register, and everybody empty their pockets." He pulled at my jacket to take it off of me. "NOW!" he demanded.

Something in my chest rose up that I didn't expect.
"No," I said calmly.
The young man was surprised, "What? What you say old man?"
"I said no," repeating my words calmly and turning to face him. "And I'm not old! I'm forty-two. I just look bad. But NO!"
"No?!" the young man questioned now pointing the gun at my face. He was blinking nervously. I don't think he expected anyone to challenge him.
"No. I'll give you some money, but you can't have all of it. It's not all mine to give."
He seemed puzzled at first but then remembered his mission, "No, but it's all mine to take, OLD MAN!" He grabbed me close by my jacket "The money and the jacket you old bastard."
I looked at the gun. It was a small revolver. I could see that it didn't have any bullets in the chambers. I laughed.
"What the hell you laughing at old man? I'll kill you right here!" I couldn't stop myself from chuckling. Tears formed in my eyes as I laughed harder.
"I mean it old man. I kill you and...and...and everybody in here."
I laughed a little harder but now on purpose. "How you gonna do that with no bullets, boy?"

I grabbed the wrist that held the gun. Then I took him quickly by the back of his neck and pulled his head down hard onto my knee. I took the gun from him before reaching out my hand to help him up. I pushed him into the booth next to the one I just left.

"Why you doing this?" I asked him. "What's going on?" He shivered and sobbed. I slid into the booth with him and put my arm around his shoulder. "What's going on?" I whispered to him.

"You don't know nothing, old man!" he said shuddering in tears.

"No, but I will if you tell me," I said gently.

He put his hand to his face. He was trying to hide his tears and I could tell his face was tender from my knee strike as well.

I turned to the young waitress, "Bring me a little bag of ice please."

The area below his left eye was beginning to swell. The waitress returned with the ice. Debbie studied the situation standing at the end of the counter with a phone in her hand.

I supposed that she was trying to decide whether to call 911 or not. I held up my hand to stay her from that call. The man slid to put his back against the wall so that he could see me and still hold the back of ice to his face.

"I lost my job. I got fired. My son...he's been sick...he's three months old. He's got meningitis and asthma. My girlfriend got the post...something...partum. I can't afford all the medication they need. We ain't got no family to help us. They just talk and fuss...and...they ain't no help. I didn't know what else to do!" His shoulders trembled, trying to restrain his grief.

"You got a record, son?"

He shook his head stammering, "N-n- no sir. No sir!"

I studied him carefully. Nothing about his posture, face, or body movements gave me any reason to think he was lying.

I remembered reading a book by an FBI guy on how our bodies often tell more truth than our mouths, especially our feet. Nothing he did or didn't do made me feel like he was being dishonest, and I chose to trust my impression of him.

"I can't give you all my money. If I could, I would. But maybe ... go to this address."

I took the receipt from the table and on the back of it, I wrote down the address to my father's church. "Go here. First, you go home and hold the baby and take care of your girlfriend."

I gave him $100. "Buy what you can with this now. Today you also ask God to forgive you and help you. Pray. Pray with your girlfriend and ask God to help you. Then you go to this church this afternoon. Tell the church office you need to speak with the pastor. Tell them Johnny Box sent you. Tell the pastor about your situation. He'll do what he can to help you."

I slid out of the booth. I reached for his hand. He took it with force and pulled himself out of the booth and stood. He hugged me, still trying to restrain his tears.

"What's your name son?"

"It's Dale. My name's Dale."

"Dale...you stay straight." I glared into his eyes. "Stay straight! You hear me?"

He nodded nervously, "Yes...yessir."

"You love that girl? What's her name?"

"Cindy...sir. Yes sir, I do," he said without hesitation.

"Then you marry Cindy. You love that woman right. You love that boy of yours right. What's his name?"

"Dale Junior."

I smiled. "You take care of Lil DJ...the best you can. And what you did this morning...you can do better than this, ok?"

Dale nodded at me, "Yes sir. I will, sir."

I studied his eyes. "I believe you will, Dale."

Dale turned to leave, defeated yet victorious.

I stopped him, "Dale?" He turned to hear me.

"You work on cars?"

"A bit," he answered matter-of-factly.

"Today, you go to Jimbo's on Ingram avenue. Tell him you're Johnny Box's guy. He'll be needing some help."

Dale teared up again. "I will. Thank you! Thank you, Mr. Johnny Box." The young man turned and left the diner.

Debbie came to stand beside me. "That was a real good thing you just did. You maybe saved three lives."

Debbie nodded. Her eyes watered as she turned, patting me on the shoulder. This was a good start to my day. I was grateful for this moment.

Debbie had one more thing to say, and so she stopped me before I opened the diner door.

"Did you just give him your job?"

"I guess I did," I answered.

"I guess you don't wanna say where you're headed to but...I wish you all the best whatever's on the other side of here."

"Thank you, Deb," I said as I turned to leave. She couldn't know how perfect those words were to me right now.

"Goodbye, John Allen Boxton."

I paused but didn't turn. No more time for words. The clock was ticking.

# Don't kill him – Kill me

I owed Duck $300. I had $337.27 in my pocket. As I drove along the city streets to the eastern edge of the city where he lived, I passed sign after sign of shops and restaurants. Duck probably hadn't eaten yet. He wasn't an early riser, and something had him worked up. I had just had a fabulous breakfast and a moment of glory. The least I could do was get my cousin something to eat.

I pulled into a drive thru. It was still only ten in the morning and breakfast would still be on the menu. I ordered Duck a chicken-egg-and-cheese biscuit. I got him some strawberry jelly packets and mustard packets. I remembered he ate a meal like this one morning when we were on a road trip a long time ago. We had gone to South Carolina for the wedding of one of his buddies from the Navy.

The sandwich and an orange juice cost $4.89. I now had $332.38. I pulled out of the drive thru and weaved through the parking lot to the light. It was a left turn, and as I sat at the light, there was an old man standing at the corner with a sign. I gave him a five-dollar bill and wished him safety and God's blessings. I dropped some change somewhere in the car as I went into my pocket. I now had $327.27.

I continued eastward down State road 50 until I found my turn off the main road. After a few more turns, I hit a dead end. I had missed a turn, but now I remembered where I was supposed to go. It wasn't long until I found the apartments Duck lived in. I knocked on the door. At first, he didn't open it, and everything suddenly got quiet beyond the door.
The door finally opened slowly, and Duck peered through the slit. His face lit up when he recognized me, and the door flew open.

"You brought me that money?" I nodded. Duck swallowed me in a hug. "Thank you bro...thank you." He released me, "C'mon in man."

"I figured you didn't eat yet. I ate at Debbie's," I said sitting the fast-food bag on the table in front of his shaggy couch.

"Thank you, man. I'm starving." Duck picked up the bag and nearly ripped it open. "Oh, man! Wow! You got me a...oh man, thank you." Duck began opening the jelly and mustard packet to prepare his sandwich the way I thought he'd like it. "Man...you remember that trip up to South Carolina?"

"I remember," I said smiling at the memories. I didn't need to go down memory lane, so decided to change the subject.

"Here, Duck." I tried to hand him the money I owed him. He was already deep into a grin and some recollection that I probably didn't want to relive.

"What was that girl's name, man?"

I just nodded, "I dunno man. We just danced together."

"Mannnn, if that was just dancing, I don't know what it woulda been like if she actually got you up to that room." Duck was smiling at me as he poured the orange juice over some ice cubes in a cup.

"But she didn't. My marriage survived that weekend," I retorted.

Duck nodded. "When was the last time you saw Julie?"

I scratched my head taking a deep breath, "Maybe...a few months."

"It's a real shame bro. I know how much y'all love each other. Shame you didn't stick." He stopped chewing and held up his hand, "Wait, did you ever sign the papers?"

I took a deep breath, "Yeah, I did – this morning." Duck sat down to enjoy his sandwich shaking his head. "Sit down, man. We need to catch up."

I didn't want to sit. I had other things and people to check off my list. "I better go man. Let me give you this..."

BAM! The door blasted open, slamming against the wall. The door wasn't locked after I came in. Two guys stepped into Duck's living room holding guns. One was very large, and the other more slender. I thought, *Maybe this is how I die. Thought I'd die in water.*

"You must be Erick," I said to the slimmer one entering the room last.

He was wearing a leather vest with no shirt underneath. His name Erick etched in some fancy font was tattooed on his chest. He looked to be in his mid-twenties and was in very athletic shape, his dirty blonde hair trimmed around the sides and the back but long on the top. The larger man was a red-head, complete with freckles. Duck and I were both long past our primes.

"Who the fuck are you?" Erick said looking me up and down. "Who is this old man, Duck?" he asked with a clear air of agitation on his face. The other guy made a move that seemed like he was flanking Duck.

I positioned myself in between Duck and the two guys. Duck was still holding half of his sandwich. Erick...man, I got your money!" Duck insisted nervously. "My ...my cousin...he came here today to pay me what I owe you."

Erick looked me over again.

I spoke like a man with nothing to lose. "I can buy his debt...he owes you $300. I owe him $300. I can just cut out the middle man and pay you." I began pulling out the money I had left over from this morning's activities. "Here, I got $327...and 27 cents," I blurted triumphantly.

Erick addressed Duck. "I'm still pissed, DUCK...pissed you had me drive all the way up here to get MY money YOU owe me...from some OTHER dude!" Erick gave me strange looks. "I need to just put some lead in your ass boy. I don't think you understand how much trouble I go to for you."

Erick tried to push me aside, but I stood my ground. Erick pushed the gun into my neck, "Move, old man!" I held up the money, "Take it all. He owes you $300. Take the twenty-seven dollars...and the twenty-seven cents too. It's yours." Erick didn't take the money from me.

He pushed the gun harder into my throat, his friend pushed me back, and then he threw me into the couch that Duck sat on. Erick pointed his gun at Duck.

I popped up in between the gun and Duck holding my hands up. "Hey man, the debt is paid. Take the money. If you gotta kill somebody, man...kill me."

Erick looked at me strangely. "This your lover, Duck? You a punk?"

Duck explained, "That's my cousin, man. He's family. He's got love for me, man. That's my keeper."

I could hear the appreciation in Duck's voice. Donald Anthony Hilliard was my cousin's name. People teased him for being clumsy when he was young, and they called him Duck. As he grew and became an athlete, he was no longer clumsy, but the name stuck.

Athletics led to him getting injured which led to pain killers which led to drugs which led to Erick. Erick's foot struck my chest. I barely saw it until it was nearly back on the floor. I was thrust violently back into the couch. "That sandwich looks delicious...DUCK!!" Erick said.

Duck held out the sandwich obediently. I wanted to knock the sandwich from Duck's hand, but Erick's friend was now holding his gun pointed firmly in my chest. If I was to be alive tomorrow, I would have had a bruise. Maybe I will still have a bruise, but since I would be dead, I don't guess I'll care.

"Erick. You like music?" I asked.

Erick looked at me sternly, "You wanna sell me some records, old man? Some cassettes? Some eight-track tapes?" He teased with sarcasm all over his face bouncing his head to accentuate his sarcasm.

I held the bills out, and then dropped them down onto the coffee table. Erick studied the cash. He counted the money out and took $300. "Take your $27 and twenty-seven cents. I ain't no thief. This ain't no robbery."

"Duck plays guitar man. He sings ...he's got a great voice. Maybe you ought to ...like be his manager." I suggested.

"Do I look like an agent, old man?" Erick retorted.
I stood up slowly.

"I heard your family was in the business. I think you look like somebody who can be whoever they wanna be."

Erick's face changed. He lowered the gun though it was still pointing at me. He put the $300 in his pocket and stepped around the coffee table to stand over Duck. "Didn't you hear me say that sandwich looked good?" He took the remaining half of the sandwich from Duck and took a bite. "Damn, Duck. This is a tasty sandwich." He quickly finished the sandwich. "I didn't know sheep ate chicken!"

Duck and I were both confused. "You're a sheep Duck. You're not a musician, Donald. You're a fucking sheep." He stood back and pointed his gun at Duck while the other guy pointed his gun at me.

"Blessed is he who in the name of charity and goodwill, shepherds the weak through the valley of darkness, for he is truly his brother's keeper and the finder of lost children. You're lost Duck. I'm gonna take you home now!" He pointed the gun at Duck's face.

I draped myself over Duck. "NOOOO," I screamed.

"Erick laughed. "Wow. This old man is gonna get shot...then I'm gonna knock his dead ass off you, and then shoot you in the face Duck. Erick lowered the gun.

I was still spreading my body over Duck, but I turned over to see Erick. My mind started racing as I thought how to change the situation. "Erick, please reconsider the music thing. Duck is already known, man. He just needs someone to stay on top of him...make sure he gets to shows. People already pay to hear him man...he just needs to show up. How you think he had money for me to borrow from him?"

Erick rubbed his chin with his free hand. "How much? How much you make at these shows Duckie Duck?"

Duck was still nervous.

"Man, GET off him! I can't talk to him with you laying all over his ass! Sit down, old man!"

I slid over to let Duck talk. I exhaled and also felt the tension easing from Duck's body. "Tell him, Duck."

"It varies. I made $3000 at one event. I made a grand doing a wedding. I got like $20 grand for a single a few years back. But it never made the radio...people liked it, but the radio didn't."

"I gotta hear something," Erick demanded.

"Right now?" Duck said nervously.

"Right fucking now...or I shoot both o' you in the face."

I started to feel like Erick never planned to shoot anyone today, only to threaten with the gun.

"Gimme a sec to get set up."

Duck slowly got up and disappeared down a hallway. Duck's dusty apartment had two bedrooms. One of his rooms in the back was essentially a studio. Erick and his friend stood, arms folded staring sternly at me as we waited. I stared sternly back.

"C'mon back," Duck commanded from elsewhere in the two-bedroom apartment. Duck got his equipment powered up. He was now standing in the middle of the room with his guitar strapped onto his shoulder. He hit a few chords to get warmed up and then started to play.

I loved listening to Duck play. He poured out all his misery about what his life could have been into his music. I leaned against the wall closing my eyes. Duck's voice was a perfect mix of smooth and raspy. He sang of regret, of disappointment, of being dependent on things that were not dependable. His guitar seemed to sing right along with him in a soft yet forceful poetic melody.

Duck finished the song and I was still standing with my eyes closed processing the beauty of his song. I was proud of Duck at this moment. I wanted to hear more.

"Damn," Erick said. "I'm in."

The mood changed and my mind quickly began looking for a way to make this moment last beyond today. I would not be here tomorrow.

"Duck. Remember that guy that was supposed to be your manager...that creepy looking dude. Didn't he give you a contract...and you were thinking about it?"

"Ahhh...yeah. I think I do."

"Go get it," I suggested. "You can just scratch out that dude's name and put Erick's name."

"Yo-yo...how much is in it for me?" Erick asked.

"Twenty percent," Duck said as he flitted out of the room sliding between Erick and the big guy. "Twenty percent of gross."

"Make it twenty-five."

Duck returned from across the hallway in his room.

"Yeah, here it is. Twenty-five is cool."

"The contract is for a year, right Duck?" I commented.

"Ahhh, yeah. A year."

"A year of making sure this lazy bum gets to his shows. Man, he could do four or five shows a week man. Ten or fifteen grand a week man...while you help him get back on the map, man. He could make some real money. The worst that can happen is somebody buys out your contract with him. It's legit work, dude."

Erick nodded. His eyes looked like he was calculating in his mind. I think he quickly understood the potential.

"People at the shows I go to...they got money to buy too man," Duck said.

"Or even better...could be no more dealing drugs for you man at all," I said rerouting the discussion away from drugs Erick's eyes were calculating again, but I wouldn't let up.

"You talk to people about buying drugs. You just talk to people about buying him now – only without cops and jail time. Like I said, I heard your family already knows people in the business. Duck is easy to sell." Now I was selling.

Erick nodded again. "Lemme see that." Erick took the contract from Duck. He sat down on a chair in Duck's studio reading it.

After a few minutes, he was done. "Gimme a pen."

"Wait a minute," I said. "Were you really gonna kill Duck? Us?" I demanded.

Erick's face frowned, "Nah. You was gonna get cracked with this pistol though if you kept pressin'."

Erick and Duck signed together, and Erick immediately started planning Duck's next gig and taking information from Duck on who he'd spoken with and so on.

"Hey Duck," I called out. Duck turned his attention to me.

"I gotta go man. You good?"

Duck grinned, came to me, and hugged me, "Thanks. I love you, bro."

We smiled at each other with satisfaction for the new deal.

"Erick!" I got Erick's attention. "Just one more thing." I remembered that today was my last day to live and that I promised myself I would overcome my fears.

"What old man?"

"You keep him off drugs – that's MY demand," I looked sternly at Erick and then Duck, "or he's no good to you."

"Deal," agreed Erick.

"Deal," Duck chimed in.

"One last thing," I said to Erick. He squinted, awaiting my words.

I swung with all my strength catching Erick on the cheekbone. He stumbled back bent over. He stood up quickly with his gun in my face with one hand, the other hand on his jaw as though he needed to check if I broke his jaw. Clearly, I didn't.

"That's for kicking me and putting a gun in our faces," I explained.

Erick relaxed and started to laugh, "Get the fuck outta here, old man, before I hit you back and you have a stroke or something."

He turned to Duck, "Don't get any ideas 'cause I let him off easy."

I nodded at Duck and he grinned back at me.

"Later, Cuz," he said.

"Later Duck," I dryly responded...knowing there would not be a later.

I left Duck's apartment feeling victorious. I'd done another amazing thing. Duck would be better off. Erick would too actually.

It was still a good day but much less of it remained, and I had people to see. I felt like Cinderella, only the Good Witch didn't give me a timer, and there was more than a fancy dress, some slippers, and party at stake.

# A Jacket to Die For

A fter leaving Duck's apartment, I had one more apartment to go to. Elliot, a guy I once called a friend. I don't really know why, but suddenly Elliot was not my friend. He stopped returning my calls and gave me angry looks the last time I saw him.

I made a couple of attempts to understand what he suddenly had against me, but he never gave me an opportunity to even ask. I didn't think it was about the jacket, but who knows. I always meant to give him the jacket, but I never remembered to bring it on the few occasions I might have seen him when we were still on speaking terms. So, now I'm making a special trip. I didn't even know for sure if he'd be at home, but I had heard he'd gotten fired from his job not long ago.

Elliot was on the north side of town, nearly to Casselberry. He lived in the bustle of the University community. It was even busier than I remembered. His apartment complex was essentially a high rise built around a huge pool. Elliot lived on the fifth floor. Loud music emanated from one of Elliot's neighbor's apartment. It was music I didn't care for; it wasn't at all like what Duck played. Duck played music that was a soft yet intense rock that spoke to my soul. The stuff I was hearing now was little more than yelling and screaming both with a guitar and without.

I knocked on the door and waited. I stood there for a moment before knocking again. Finally, the door opened... well it parted from the door frame. No light from the hallway seemed to penetrate the darkness in the room.

A shadowy figure stood silently in the partly opened door. Finally, the shadow-person spoke.

"Box-man...Johnny Box. C'mon in, bro," the shadowy figured signed with only mildly feigned salutations. He smelled of alcohol so deeply that the bottle held clutched in his hand could scarcely explain the odor. The apartment stank of old trash that assailed my nose as I entered the dark apartment.

"O-o-old Johnny Box... Gooood old, Johnny Box!"

I entered his apartment removing the jacket to hand it to him. "I wanted to return your..." my eyes widened as I turned to speak with him face to face. The last thing I saw was the bottle coming at my head before everything went black. My last thought was, *Maybe I should have died with the jacket.*

I awoke tied to a chair. The music was still blasting only now I also felt the music. Every drumbeat, every violent strum of the guitar was like a lash to the side of my head. I wondered if I was bleeding. The room was still dark and smelly, but now it felt like a fog hung in the air.

Elliot was doing something behind me. There was something in my mouth. My wrists were bound to the arm of a chair, and my legs were tied to the chair also. I tried to stand, thinking I could get into a bent-over position and maybe swing the chair to break the back legs. Then the front legs would likely split when I sat down onto the floor.

The chair was rudely slammed to the floor, "Sit back down, loverboy!"

I was confused and turned to look at Elliot with this same confusion on my face. He yanked a smelly t-shirt out of my mouth to allow me to speak. My mouth felt weird and I had a compulsion to lick my lips and roll my bottom jaw.

"What's going on Elliot? Why did you hit me? Why did you tie me up?"

"You KNOW what you did, you son of a bitch!" Elliot proclaimed. "And I'm not letting you put your hands on ME, Mr. Wrestling champ."

I felt my eyebrow lurch to a high position, and this also hurt.

"Admit it! You RUINED my life!" Elliot was pacing, "And for what?"

"What are you talking about Elliot? I'm not here to hurt you."

A shiny pocket-knife was suddenly at my throat. "What am I talking about?" The knife pressed hard into my throat. "I should just slit you now!"

"Look, man, I'm sorry it took me this long to return your jacket. If I knew you'd be this upset about it, I would've never borrowed it in the first place!"

"Jacket? JACKET!!! You think I'd be petty enough to wanna kill you over a JACKET!" The knife flickered in the dark and I felt something hit my arm.

"I'm pissed...I'm not stupid, Johnny."

"You slept with my GIRL!" Elliot put the knife in his left hand so that his right could swing freely. I felt a hard thud as his fist hit my left jaw. At least this time I could flinch, maybe keep him from breaking my jaw. He apparently wasn't satisfied. He followed the blow to my head with more blows to my stomach and chest. "You slept with my girl!"

I recovered and looked up at Elliot, "What girl?" "WHAT GIRL?"

Elliot sent another shot to my stomach. "You got a beautiful wife, but that's not enough for you!"

Elliot was pacing now but then stopped to give me a backhand to the right side of my face. The room tilted sideways slightly.

"Redhead, amazing smile, even more amazing eyes and body!" He pushed my head using the butt end of the pocket-knife. "Ring a bell now?"

"About 3 months ago? At the Rock festival?" I asked.

"Bingo, you son of a BITCH!" he said, pounding my ribs again with his balled-up right hand. He paced the room and hit me again in the ribs when he came back, stepping into a full swing. I felt it through my entire torso.

"I never touched her!" I exclaimed after coughing to get my breath again.

"Liar!!" Elliot hit me again two or three times more in my midsection. He hit me so hard with the last blow it knocked not only the wind out of me but also knocked the chair backward. I struggled to breathe. Elliot was pacing the room again now. "I am gonna... kill you... I swear!"

Having my knees up, still tied to the chair now on the floor helped my diaphragm to relax some. Elliot was standing over me now.

"Gimme a second. I'll....I'll tell you," I said still trying to gather myself. "That girl was trouble man...I thought she was there with you at first."

Elliot kneeled down with the knife now in his right hand, the point resting on my dress shirt which covered my hero t-shirt. I wasn't feeling much like a hero now.

"I was standing with my cousin, one of the musicians at the festival. People were crowding him to get his signature, and they pushed me away from him. She came up to me and asked if I knew him. I told her I did. She asked if I could get a picture of him with her. She looked back at you like she was about to call you, but you were talking to some other girl. Man...you should'a seen her face when she saw you talking to that other girl. I wasn't sure if she was with you or not then."

Elliot pushed the knife down a bit into my shirt. I could feel the point about to break my skin. I couldn't help but flinch.

"So, it's MY fault you fucked her?"

"What? No...I told you I never touched her?" I insisted.

"I took her to the back to meet the musician!" Elliot waited for me to continue. "She asked me my name. I told her. Then I got her to Duck's room, and I introduced her. They talked and I left."

I took a breath as more of the details of that night came to me, "I didn't think much of it but when I left, she said 'It was nice to meet you, Duck!' I was like...why'd she call me Duck? But I just left the room instead of correcting her." I nodded. "She must have thought Duck had my name!"

Elliot started crying. "She was gone for HOURS! Then she showed up at my apartment like two in the morning. We had sex, but she called out YOUR name...Oh, Johnny BOX."

Elliot sat down shaking in tears. "I wasn't flirting with that other girl. I knew her from work! She worked at a different branch of my accounting firm, and she was in town."

"Man...I'm sorry Elliot. I really am man." I shook my head. "But...honestly man, if you saw that expression she had on her face after she thought you WERE flirting...that woman is crazy...I think maybe...maybe she just went with Duck to hurt you, man. And, Duck...he doesn't even know you."

I tried to think how I would feel if Julie had done to me what Elliot's girlfriend had done to him. I was still in pain from all the abuse Elliot had given me, but I felt pain in my heart for him. I know that love for a woman can drive a man crazy.

"What happened to you man?" I asked.

Elliot sobbed and fell back onto the floor with his knife hand on his forehead. "I started drinking...a lot. One day I blew up at my boss. He fired me. That was weeks ago. I'm outta money. I drank all my hard liquor. I got ran out of bars. I drank up all my money in beer. When you showed up, I was just gonna kill you and then kill myself."

"Wow man. I thought you were gonna kill me...but I thought you were gonna kill me over this jacket!"

I looked over at Elliot again, "Hey man, you gonna untie me?"

Elliot chuckled, wiping tears from his eyes. "Yeah...yeah. Just a sec." Elliot gathered himself before coming to kneel over me. He used the pocketknife to cut the layers of duct tape woven around my wrists and ankles.

"So, now what? I hope you aren't gonna try to kill the other guy!"

Elliot began sobbing again, "No...no...you were right. She was a crazy BITCH!" He began to shake. "I ruined my life over a crazy whore. Now, what am I supposed to do?" He seemed to get the depth of the situation even more. "I almost killed you man...over ...over a misunderstanding!"

Elliot stood up, wiping his face again. He helped me up. "Man, I am sooo sorry." He used his shirt to dry his face. "All this time...you tried to call me to find out what was going on...man. I feel like a real ass!"

I nodded. "Well, you were that...and probably more." I laughed, "But hey... I'm still alive. I'm banged up, but I'm still alive."

I thought this was going to be the end of me. There was nothing heroic about dying tied up in a chair on the floor. I started taking the jacket off, aggravating the bruises and soreness just caused by my old friend.

He began helping me get the jacket off. "I really should let you keep it, bro."

I was surprised Elliot would call me bro after all this. "Nah...It's yours. Besides, I'm not gonna need it."

"Ok," Elliot said.

"Can I sit down?" I asked.

"Oh...yeah...yeah, man." Elliot helped me to a leather chair in the dark of his apartment. It was one of the few pieces of furniture not covered in garbage or dirty clothes.

"What am I gonna do, man?" Elliot said standing by the glass sliding door leading to his balcony.

I thought for a moment, "Hey, you're an accountant, right?"

"I was 'till a few weeks back," Elliot answered, not turning around to face me.

"That shop I used to work at...I kinda helped him with his books. He could really use some professional help though. In fact, if he likes you, he can easily connect you with some rich guys that might also need help."

I wasn't sure if it was a good idea to put Elliot in connection with any sort of criminal element, but it was all I had at this moment to change his trajectory. Besides, I trusted Jimbo to guide anyone in dealing with his shadowy clientele like he protected me. Elliot sat on the floor, his back against his T.V. stand.

"Man, you gonna do all this for me...even after I threatened your life!"

I honestly felt no ill will towards Elliot. "Man, life is too short to be carrying around unnecessary baggage. That goes for you and that crazy girl of yours."

Elliot chuckled, "Yeah, I know. Easy for you to say. You never had lady troubles like me man."

Elliot hadn't been paying much attention the past few years, I guess. I wasn't going to explain it to him. "Elliot, what I want you to do man...figure out how to love yourself. You do that first. Women will be drawn to you...people, in general, will be drawn to you."

I thought about what I was saying, and it was a sudden epiphany. "I think it has something to do with negative versus positive energy. When you have positive energy, people feed off of it. If you got negative energy, only more negative energy people can feed off you...or maybe people that are healers and need to give would be drawn to you maybe."

Elliot nodded, "Makes sense."

"Go talk to Jimbo today, bro," I suggested.

"You gonna be there?" Elliot asked.

"Nah, I got stuff to do. Don't wait on me man. Just tell him I sent you. While you're at it...go talk to my pops also at the church. You need to talk to somebody to help you figure out how to love you man."

I struggled to stand up. I was feeling every bruise and every knot. I truly felt love for Elliot. I hoped he would be able to turn his life around. I finally stood with Elliot's help.

"Can I hug you, man?" Elliot asked. I grabbed him and pulled him close despite all the shooting pain.

"Ain't gotta ask, bro."

Elliot began sobbing again, "You saved my life man. I was gonna end it today, man. When you knocked on that door, man....I was sharpening this knife to cut my throat man. I been thinking about it for a week and today...today was about to be the day."

Elliot struggled to speak and then regained himself somewhat. "When I saw you, I was like...I'm gonna kill him first, and THEN I'm gonna do it." He shook his head. "Man, if you waited like another hour...I don't think I would be here, man."

I smiled thinking of God and my superhero shirt. I hugged Elliot harder, "Love you, bro." *I can still die well*, I thought, *Cinderella Man*.

Elliot helped me to the stairs after I hugged him and told him I loved him again. He was surprised to hear that I am sure. He hugged me back even harder, and I felt water on my neck. His face was wet with tears when he stepped back. All he could do was nod at first.

Time was really slipping away quickly, but I couldn't seem to put the car into drive. I needed to spend a little time digesting all that just happened.

Aside from feeling like I just got my butt kicked, which I did, I felt really satisfied. I felt at peace despite my predicament. That event with Duck was the only event of his I ever went to. I had asked Elliot, who never really comes out, to come. It took a company event for him to come to something I would normally not ever attend.

Not only did he come, his coworker came which caused his nutty girlfriend to show her true colors. I was almost sad about what happened to my friend Elliot, but it could be worse. He could have married her.

As far as his job situation goes, he would likely end up becoming an accountant for some very highly paid people, and he might actually make more money...a lot of money. I realized that the situation seemed desperate to him right now, but I felt like he would actually be in a much better place in a year from now...even six months from now. Some time back, I tried to tell him to leave the other job because they were not paying him well, and he hated his boss. In my opinion, the girlfriend never seemed right for him.

I couldn't say this to him, but I felt happy for him anyway. I did tell him that things could only get better from here. That seemed to comfort him. I felt God's hand at work in all of this. I felt oddly free of the fact that I still knew I would die today. I had done something good and I was thankful for that.

I recalled that on the way down the hallway, I looked into one of the apartment windows and saw a television commercial that said: "Make Peace not war." I knew that message was for me and I felt like I was doing just that. I hoped it was enough for me to get a second chance.

# A Final Gift

Now off to see Lilliard – Lilliard, the ladies' man. He wanted to learn how to fix cars but was too busy selling whatever he sold for a living. He was also an ex-football player. He had broad shoulders, blonde hair and great teeth. He had a perfect chin and riveting blue eyes sitting atop his six-foot-four-inch slender frame. Ladies loved him everywhere he went...especially at the gym, I understand.

I hoped he would be at home as I didn't have his phone number. So, I drove to his condominium in the downtown area. I assumed he was staying close to his clients, which were restaurants, clubs and bars...if I understood what I heard.

The downtown area was also his prowling grounds. When I saw his car out front, I was relieved. I was also excited that I would see him after such a long time. I hadn't seen him since my anniversary party with Julie. Lilliard, nicknamed Lil or Lillie, was neither small enough to be called "Lil" or feminine enough to be Lillie. He was secure enough in himself to be called either or simply Lilliard. He was gorgeous, smart, and yet down to earth and everyone wanted to be around him...except men with young wives or young girlfriends.

I collected the box gingerly. At first, I tried resting it on my right hip under my arm, but that area was tender on my right side. So, I carefully shifted it to my left hip before ringing the doorbell.

A short while later the door became ajar, "What's a matter babe, forget your ke.." An amazing looking brunette stood in the doorway. She was wearing a nightgown that was opened in the front revealing a good bit of her full breasts and rather skimpy panties. She quickly covered up, "Sorry, I thought you were Lil. He, like, just left on his bike to get me some spinach for my smoothie."

"I'm sorry ma'am," I'm Johnny. I'm his uncle...step-uncle...ex-step uncle."

The woman's eyebrows furrowed while she waited for me to decide exactly what my relationship with Lillie was.

After an uncomfortable pause, I continued. "I have something for him."

"You want me to give it to him?" she asked.

I didn't want to leave it to chance. I also wanted him to know where it came from. I wanted to see his expression. Also, today, what remained of it, was my last day alive. I wanted to say good-bye.

"I'll wait...in the car," I said stammering a bit. The woman was beautiful even just from a peek through a partially open door. But she was likely half my age and I was married...sort of...so I tried to honor my wife, ex-wife and not gawk at the woman. I turned to take a seat in my car.

"That's crazy," she said. "What would your nephew think of me if I made you wait in the car. You're his family, right?"

I nodded.

"Come on in," the door drifted open and I entered.

"I'm Clarice," she introduced herself.

"I'm Johnny, Uncle Johnny."

"It's nice to meet you, Uncle Johnny. I was about to take a bath but let me put some clothes on, and I'll be right out."

I stepped inside the foyer. I caught sight of a large oval mirror to my right. I faced the mirror to see myself, perhaps for the last time. I tucked in my shirt and tried to brush the wrinkles out of it. I was glad I had shaved and put on my best jeans and shiny shoes. This was the best I had looked in many months, once you ignored my face and all the bruises.

I heard a faucet creak from being turned off faintly in the background. I heard water cease running just underneath some soft jazz playing from someplace remote in the condo. I sat on Lillie's leather couch. He seemed to have very good taste in decorating...either that or he had very tasteful feminine help.

Everything was very well put together in his apartment. There was lots of natural light and it smelled...it smelled clean, a stark contrast from Elliot's place.

"Are you that uncle that builds cars for a living?" she asked from another room.

"That's me!" I called out.

"Uncle Johnny then?"

"Yes," I confirmed.

She finally returned to the main room to entertain me. She eyed the box I was carefully holding. "What's in the box?" she asked before stifling herself, "Sorry, that's none of my business."

I smiled, "It's ok. Lillie loved my car collection. I wanted him to have it."

"That's really nice. You going someplace?"

I paused thinking of how to answer. "Well...it's just time for him to have it," I said dodging the question.

"That's not really an answer, but I'll let you slide," she said perceptively with an innocent smile.

The door opened, "Hey babe!" the woman said standing, almost bouncing to the front door. "SHIT!" I shifted in my seat to see what upset her.

Suddenly, the woman's demeanor changed. "Bob! What are you doing here?" she shouted. "We're done!"

I turned around. There was an older man standing just inside from the foyer—a little older than me. He was extremely well dressed and the shine from his shoes was hard to ignore. Two large men came in behind the man and walked towards me. I stood up to face them, sliding in front of the one nearest Lillard's girlfriend.

"This the piece o' shit old man you screwing around on me for?" the man said with a strong Italian accent.

This began to feel like the moment the whole day was leading up to. I never felt like Elliot was going to kill me. I never thought Duck's dealer actually wanted to kill anyone. But this guy...he reminded me of the men that brought their cars to Jimbo's shop. They were all quiet, calculating men whose very auras spoke of death.

I quickly decided I would accept my death if it meant my wife's beloved nephew would be spared. "Leave her out of this!" I demanded. "GET THE HELL OUT OF MY HOUSE!" I yelled. One of the large men blocked my way from the well-dressed Italian.

The large man in front of me grabbed my throat in his gargantuan hand. I took hold of his thumb and bent it backwards as hard as I could. It didn't work nearly as well I expected. He was supposed to fully release me in shock and pain. Instead, it was only enough to let me step out of his grip and deliver a vicious right cross. It hurt to swing, but I swung with all the strength I could muster.

The man bent over but didn't fall. He smiled at me and grabbed my left shoulder. Next, the very air between my body and this man's fist seemed to gather and move out of the way. When his fist hit my stomach, it felt like a construction event. It felt like something that had been in place for many years was suddenly torn down by a single blow of heavy machinery. My heels left the ground immediately followed by my knees buckling. I was on the floor and pain radiated from my ribs in every direction.

"Take him to the bathroom," I heard the well-dressed man say in a strong accent. This time, I could not even look up at him.

"Bob...don't kill him! Please...please...please," Clarice pleaded.

I wanted to say something to reinforce that I was her boyfriend and not my wife's beautiful young nephew. I didn't want him to not be beautiful anymore or worse. My death on a foretold day would be one thing. I didn't want my wife...ex-wife to suffer the loss of the family's prized son. But I couldn't speak.

I was still stunned. My muscles were unresponsive as I was dragged across the floor.

"Hold it," the well-dressed man commanded. His thug stopped dragging me and the well-dressed man was now standing over me. His shiny shoes were not as shiny on the bottom. I got one very quick look at the bottom of his shoe before the world became a red haze.

"Let's go." I heard him say to his ruffian.

The pains in my head returned only with a muffled deafness in my left ear. Now I couldn't make sense of what was being said either about me or on my behalf. This was it. My death approached. I wanted to see my father. I wanted to see my wife. I wanted to give the car to my friend that I had cheated. I wanted to say I was sorry to each of them.

I saw my son...my stillborn son. He was as real in my hands as the aches in my head. I saw Julie crying. The doctors had tried to save him, but they failed. And now all there was left was to say goodbye to a dream we had. It was the moment my marriage fell apart even though it limped along for some tortured years. I never forgave God for my son dying. I somehow even blamed Julie. I think I blamed God and my father for my mother's death. I wanted to say I was sorry to all of them for carrying around all that grief and bitterness.

I wanted to see my son now. I hoped God had kept him for me. I hoped I could hold him again. I would not get to hold his mother...the very love of my life.

"They ran the tub? How convenient. Don't gotta make a mess or nothing. Put him in," ordered the well-dressed man to his oversized minions.

I could hear, though muffled. I could see I was being picked up to be put into the tub that had been prepared for Clarice's bath. I tried to resist. I felt my hands being ripped away from the tub's edges and a massive hand pressed on the back of my head. Another hand pinned one of my arms behind my back with an unfamiliar cruelty. Even the pain dealt upon my body by Elliot did not compare to the vileness I was being put through now. There was no pleasure in what Elliot had planned to do to me. There was not even malice. It was more like ...justice, though wrong in his judgment.

This was different. This man that now began the process of ending my life in pain and horror...he enjoyed it. He enjoyed hurting me. His boss enjoyed watching me hurt.

My day had begun with me dreaming I would die. I remembered waking in a puddle of water. The prophecy was now complete despite my fighting against it. Who was I to resist the very will of God? I was no one. The hand on the back of my neck emphatically reminded me as I gagged water into my lungs. It was the most terrible feeling I'd ever known.

Suddenly I was released. I fell backward out of the tub coughing water out of my lungs and mouth. I saw the beautiful young lady also falling back away from the tub soaked from head to her midsection. Her breasts heaved as she tried to refill her lungs with air and coughed to empty them of water.

I could hear police barking orders at the men. I sat against the wall, relieved and trying to regain my full senses. Lillie sprang into the bathroom and picked up the young woman to embrace her.

He looked down at me, "Uncle Johnny?"
I nodded.
"What are you doing here?" he asked.
It seemed to take me forever to be able to speak. "Wanted to bring you something." My upper body slipped sideways down the side of the wall, reeling in pain from the top of my head to my neck and again from my right shoulder to my midsection. Pain emanated from those places on my body and though I was grateful I was not dead, death seemed like a merciful release from the pain I felt.

A police officer opened my eyes wider and spoke to me. I heard him speaking to me, and I understood his words, but I could not force my mouth to respond. I felt my mouth open slowly but no words came out. I stopped trying to speak and let my eyes close. I focused on breathing through the pain that wracked my body. Every breath hurt.

He held up fingers and I knew he wanted me to count them. After the first couple of combinations, I managed to speak.

"Four. Three. One. Five." The officer nodded. I closed my eyes again.

"Where you hurtin' buddy?" the officer asked.

"Head.... shoulder... ribs."

I overheard the officer asking questions of Clarice. She frantically explained as much as she could. I eventually felt well enough to stand with help. It still hurt to breathe, and my head was still pounding. The officer lifted my right arm which responded with a violent shooting pain throughout the right side of my body. I felt my shoulder slip back into the correct place. It had been since my second season of wrestling that I felt the pain of a dislocated shoulder. The pain was familiar like an old friend that still looked the same. It felt the same.

I wanted to cry. I slid back down against the wall. I told myself to just breathe. I was finally able to move my arm to rub my midsection. I tried again to stand.

Another of the officers returned to the bathroom and helped me out to the main room.

"So... let me get this straight – You come to visit your ...your ex-wife's nephew...outta the blue. He ain't here. You wait. Some goons show up to kill him. They mistake you for him and your first instinct is...is to take his place?"

"I guess so," seemed to be the best way to answer.

The officer nodded. "You probably saved his life...and hers."

He tried to help me to a seat, but I didn't want to sit down. It might be hard to get up, and I still had things to do today.

"You gave your nephew time to get in and see what was going on. He had the mind to call 911. It just so happened a bunch of us were parked on the next street over having a little meeting." He patted me gently on my left arm. "In my book...you're a hero, man."

That was nice to hear. I felt very satisfied. Lilliard helped me to walk through the front door of his condo. There was now a huge ruckus outside. Two paramedic vehicles were outside. The single step down from his front porch took some adjustments.

"I got you, Unc." Lilliard was very gentle. "You came all the way out here to give me your car collection?"

I took a deep, painful breath. "Yup." I leaned back against the Rambler Rebel I was nearly finished with.

He took a long look at the car. "This that same car you been working on for years?"

"Yup," I answered.

"Thank you, Uncle Johnny, ...and thank you for pretending to be me." He paused. "Why'd you do that? They could'a killed you."

"Felt right," was all I really could muster. I wanted to tell him that I loved him because I loved his aunt. I loved anything she loved. I was proud of everything she was proud of. Protecting him was my last expression of protecting her. That's why kid, I thought to myself. I didn't think he'd understand it. I am not sure even I would have yesterday.

Today, everything was crystal clear. Everything I loved. Everything I could do without. Today, I lived without hesitation and it made me feel free. So, I guess that was another reason I was willing to take his place. I needed to. I didn't have a need to die for him, but I did have a need to decide...on my own terms and live with the result...or die with it.

I looked over Lilliard's shoulder. His girlfriend sitting on the stretcher waiting for the paramedics to release her. "Ditch the girl, kid. Pretty girl...but not worth it."

A paramedic came to me; he asked me a series of questions. He looked at the cut over my eye and bruises I could feel. I told him one of the big guys dislocated my shoulder, and that it seemed to slide back into place when one of the officers tried to help me up.

They gave me an instant ice pack for my head and fashioned a sling made with a bunch of ice packs for my shoulder. They suggested I go to the hospital for stitches to treat the cut over my eye and to clean the wound. But it had stopped bleeding already.

I was given a strong pain killer and they put antiseptic on my cut. I didn't have time to go to the hospital...not for stitches to a wound that wasn't bleeding any more. Lillie sent his girlfriend to get me some liquid skin spray and between that and the ice pack, I was satisfied. I refused further care. I said good-bye to Lilliard and his girlfriend and carefully slid down into my Rambler Rebel AMC machine parked on the street.

I pulled the list out of my pocket slowly, carefully, painfully. It was wet but I could still read it. Next was supposed to be going to see my father but I only knew where Ricky worked. I didn't know where he lived nor did I have his phone number. It was time to change plans. I had $27 left in my pocket. That should be enough to get a taxi ride over the bridge to my father's house. I decided to give the car back next. I had to give the pumpkin carriage back, and I knew my time was still running out.

I now remembered something the gangster type whispered in my ear as the police dragged him out of the bathroom. He told me I was on borrowed time. He told me today would be my day no matter what. I didn't know if the well-dressed Italian man was going to be the end of me or not, but when I heard him say that my time was overdue, I believed him. But maybe I had convinced God to let me live with my deeds.

I only knew that I had more deeds to do in case my life was really going to be over today. I shifted the car into drive and headed off on my way to give back the car that I loved for five years, lying to myself that it was mine. It was no good to me where I was going, and I needed to be free of it...free of things that had to be needed.

# Vengeance is Mine

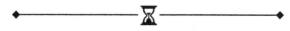

I reached the end of the street and sat at the stop sign. I felt frustrated with the three men that wanted to kill my nephew – my wife's nephew – my ex-wife's nephew. I had stopped watching the news long ago because it just seemed like crooked leaders or politicians and wealthy people continued to get away with crime after crime. It seems as though there are rules for most people to follow that the wealthy and empowered people never need to observe.

These men would have ended my life, ended Lilliard's girlfriend's life, ended Lilliard's life—even taking pleasure in the act. These men were no strangers to doing acts of evil. I imagined it was a way of life for them. I thought about men bringing their expensive cars to Jimbo for repairs or upgrades or for other things that I did without knowing more than just the work needing to be done. When evil men are determined to do wrong, who will stand up to them? Who will force them to follow the rules that common folk obey? Why are they not accountable to the same laws as me?

I recalled a man that bullied me in high school and after. He bullied my ex-wife. My anger grew. The three men that would have taken my life this day were in the hands of the police even if only temporarily. But there was one man; a man for whom I now bear ill will. He now seemed to represent an opportunity to take my frustration of these killers and apply it where it could be applied. I knew a man who deserved some vengeance to be exacted upon him. At this moment, I did not fear him. I only wanted him to know the pain he inflicted upon others. My shoulder throbbed. My head hurt. My ribs hurt but I knew that my muscles and joints would only stiffen as the day went along. I felt more anger than physical pain. I knew someone that needed to feel pain; someone that deserved to feel pain.

The pain in my shoulder only fueled my anger at the man that had stained some of my memories with my ex-wife. He was a man who chipped away at my masculinity in front of my wife. Today, he was going to suffer. I grunted through the pain I felt and shifted the car into gear. I clutched the steering wheel with my right hand instead of my left in defiance of the pain I felt throughout much of my body.

I only knew him as "Dooley." I believed I knew where he lived. He was no more than ten minutes away. After a few turns, a bit of reality hit me. This man was physically larger and stronger than me. Pure anger may not be enough to exact my vengeance upon him. People say things like, it's not the size of the dog in the fight that matters but the size of the fight in the dog. I had more fight in my mind than in my body and Dooley was a BIIIIIIG dog.

I pulled into a convenience store. Each stab of pain I felt getting out of the car was channeled into my anger towards the man I called Dooley.

I reached into my pocket, pulling out two dollars, "Give me four rolls of pennies."

The attendant looked at me strangely. "Four of 'em?"

"Four," I confirmed crisply.

"But I don't have..." I cut him off. "Four. You got 'em."

I waited, maintaining eye contact.

"Ok," the attendant relented uncomfortably.

He set them onto the counter lined up. "Four rolls of pennies."

I grabbed them, feeling awful pain and even stronger anger and left the store with the rolls of pennies in my pockets, two in each.

I slid back into the car, still defying my pain. Shifting the car into gear and backing out of the parking spot, I focused my mind on the man who held my head under the water with his cruel hand. I remembered him saying to me, "GET IN THERE, PUNK!" It fueled my anger more. I clenched my teeth together and the miles between me and Dooley made me even more frustrated. I wanted to hurt Dooley for the man he was — for the man he had been to me and others. I imagined that he still terrorized people for no other reason than that he could. Today, the world would at least have a break from Dooley—a well-deserved respite from his bitterness and evil.

At last, time and distance gave way to my intentions and I pulled up alongside the curb that I believed was the house where Dooley lived. I opened the car door and slid out feeling my ribs complicating every breath. I carefully stood and leaned back against the car that would soon no longer be mine. I was reeling in pain, awash in anger. I gathered my breath along with my anger and determination.

My lips tightened and my eyes narrowed to slits. My teeth clenched hard against all the pain I felt as I welled it up intent on unleashing it upon Dooley. Dooley was a bully to everyone and anyone he could prop himself up against and I wanted to let him know he was wrong before I died.

My body relented to my will and I stood. I came around the car and approached the front porch. There was a screened door barring the front entrance that was opened, "DOOLEY? YOU THERE?" I barked.

I stood on the first step to the porch. "DOOLEY! COME OUT!" I now had a roll of pennies in each hand. I intended to land at least four solid blows that left dents in Dooley's face or body. I expected the coin wrappers to burst but after the four rolls were spread out on the ground, I would use anything available and within reach to continue teaching Dooley a lesson. A dark figure became visible through the screen door.

"You looking for Mr. Chambers? Nicknamed Dooley?" A large woman opened the door. She had a look of calm awareness on her face. She was as tall as me and had broad shoulders. She appeared to be a physically capable woman.

"I AM," I said restraining my generated rage.

"You got some kinda beef with Mr. Chambers?" she asked, leaning against the door frame folding her arms.

"I DO!" I declared, remembering for the first-time what Dooley's last name was.

"It's been a long time coming. He's a racist and an ass and today he and I are gonna settle up." I thought using the racist label would entreat the woman to my cause.

Each of my fists clutched their own roll of pennies threatening to break the wrappers before they even connected with some part of Dooley's body.

She nodded. "Mr. Chambers was a bastard all his life…both literally AND figuratively." She nodded. "I am quite sure he hates the fact that a black woman cleans his butt and keeps him alive. And I find satisfaction in that because he can't do a thing about it. But… if all I do is remind him that God doesn't like the way he lived then I'm good with that. But you also will know what God don't like."

"Miss, I watched Dooly be a racist and a bully …to me and to others and I never did anything about it. Today, I need to do something," I explained. I almost smiled at her words until she unloaded something that sounded like don't be a hypocrite. I thought calling him a racist would soften her to my cause. I was angry with myself for allowing him to bully me, but I never did the things he did.

He was a weak man for needing to stand on others to elevate himself. I should have pitied Dooley for his weakness, but I was too angry. Today, he was going to pay for being himself.

Dooley needed to look down on people, perhaps to feel better about himself. I should have pitied Dooley for his weakness, but I was too angry.

"You gonna let me in?" I asked.

Her lips pinched to the side studying me.

"He's over there," she motioned her head to the left.

There was a shell of a man in a wheelchair slumped over but looking over at us, breathing through an oxygen mask.

"I think God took his vengeance on Mr. Chambers long before you decided to come here." She motioned towards Dooley again, "Go on. Make your peace with him now. I'm sure he deserves whatever you SAY to him but don't put your hands on him," she pointed sternly at me.

She put enough emphasis on the word to let me know that my most appropriate tool of administering justice was going to be done by my words and she would tolerate nothing more. I was left on the front porch along with a blob of something people once called Dooley.

The woman called out to me from the dark of the house, "He can hear you. Just can't talk back or move."

I heard the water turn on again and a brushing sound. The woman was cleaning something. I barely recognized Dooley. He was a mess. I didn't care what condition he developed that led him to this state. He was once a large, imposing white man with a near-permanent scowl. Now he was a blob of skin in a chair. He looked up at me from behind his oxygen mask sitting on the corner of the front porch watching the world that he once terrorized pass him gladly by. I could still see the anger in his eyes. I no longer wanted to hurt him. I didn't feel sorry for him either. I stood over him studying his wasted flesh.

"You were a waste of man all your life Dooley...now you even look like it."

My hands relaxed and I put the penny rolls on the porch railing. "This is what you deserved, a beating from someone who would no longer tolerate your abuse to the world. I'll leave these here. I want you to see them – I want you to see that the world wants you to be in the state that you're in now...because you earned this. You earned this ending to your life with the way you treated people."

The woman stepped out onto the porch now holding a cup something hot.

"So, you really ok with looking after this piece of garbage of a man?" I asked.

She nodded as she pondered her response. "I knew of him from years back. He mistreated my sister at work. She ended up quitting. I knew of him myself at the Junior college. I just...I remember watching him in the pavilion. I was studying nursing and he...I don't know what he was doing there." She studied the piled flesh of a man. "I knew something was wrong with him. He was awful to everybody."

She nodded almost laughing. "When they assigned the case to me last year and I saw him...I thought...Lord...Lord, you MUST be testing me with this one." She shook her head, "At first he was mean with his mouth. Then he couldn't talk anymore, and he was mean just with his eyes. Now...he's just mean-spirited. I think that's all he has left...his bitterness and loneliness." She turned to me, "You came here for vengeance. Romans twelve and nineteen says..."

I cut her off. "I know the scripture. ...for it is written, vengeance is mine. I will repay says the Lord."

I found her face in approval. "You know your scripture, huh?" she said in consent.

I explained, "People thought I was gonna be a preacher one day. I thought so too...a long time ago."

She nodded in silence for a short time. I assumed she was considering my words.

"I guess we all got to come to grips with what God got in store for us. And we all got a consequence for disobedience...we don't know when the good Lord will decide enough is enough...until he shows us it is. Then it's too late."

"So, you're calling me a hypocrite?" I asked, wanting to clarify what she was saying.

"You been through a lot mister. I believe I could see that even without all the bruises." She took a sip from her cup.

"I pray for that man over there. I pray for him every day...not because I like him but because God loves him. I believe God had enough of his cruelty, though. And thank God he wasn't born a rich man with that attitude he's got, or he could hurt a lot more people. He is actually beyond racist. He doesn't really like anybody...not even himself. But God still loves him and wants him to do better. So, in my obedience to the Lord, I pray for him."

"Luke. Luke six and twenty-seven," I paused before uttering the words that would condemn me of disobedience. "...love your enemies, do good to those that hate you." Now I felt small. I leaned against a support post on the front porch.

She took a deep breath. "I'm not judging you, mister. I got my own issues to deal with." She nodded pondering her next words, "This man, I believe in my heart, raped my niece." Her eyes began to water.

"He put something in her coffee, got her in a back room, made it look like she passed out drinking. He had pictures of her with liquor - said he'd been finding bottles in the trash. He even planted little bottles in different trash cans around the facility. My niece never drank a drop in her life. Her daddy died of being an alcoholic...just like he will. She didn't believe in touching it – scared the mess out of her."

She took another deep breath, "Sooooo, she got fired for drinking on the job...after he raped her."

The woman shook her head, "So, when they brought me this case I cried. I said nope...no way. That night I heard from the Lord...and I knew I was supposed to keep him."

Now, she had a faint smile—a look of satisfaction. "What I found out is that he is miserable. He WANTS to die. He DID try a few months back—just made his situation worse. Now he can't even talk. But I won't let him off that easy. He's gonna live ...as long as I can keep him alive."

"I read the bible to him every day. I take him to parks and different places...I let him see what he's missing out on because of all his evil. I don't know if he'll ever change his mind. My guess is he's going to hell when he dies...but it won't be because I didn't do what I was supposed to do...trying to help him be a better person...in his heart. I forgave him but that don't mean I'll forget what he did."

She took a sip of her drink, "Sometimes I just sit right down in front of him and laugh. And I know it ain't right...but I'm enjoying myself with him."

We looked over at him...Dooley was drooling.

"He wants to curse me out. But he can't even do that now. God will get you in the worst way when he decides to pay you back for all your evil."

She stood up straight and pointed to me, "Whatever you came over here to do, I ain't exactly sure you in any shape to do it, but you sure were determined to do it *today*." She studied me further.

"You doing some kinda bucket list, hmph?"

I smiled, careful not to laugh for the sake of my ribs.

"Maybe," I said, taking a shallow breath.

"You need someone to pray for you too mister," she said in an accusing tone.

I nodded and stepped gingerly down from the front porch. "Feel free," I said stepping carefully down the steps.

I stepped alongside the porch until I stood near where Dooley sat in his wheelchair. She was right. What I came here to do wasn't at all what God would approve of. I stared at Dooley. He stared at me. I let all the anger I felt earlier slip away. I could see he was suffering – likely for the life he lived.

"You'll never see me again. I forgive you, Dooley – for all your evil...not for you but for me. I'm free of you. I won't carry my anger towards you anymore - I don't carry anything about you anymore." I put the last two rolls of pennies on the railing.

"It's not in you to be a better man. I don't think you're going to heaven, Dooley – but...that's between you and God. Maybe you can get right with Him before you die."

Dooley began drooling again. His eyes fixed on my face. I could see his anger smoldering behind his dead eyes. I kept my back to Dooley as a walked away. I returned to my Rebel and prepared myself to slide down into the car again. I would reclaim my aids, the ice packs and sit still in the car and allow the ice packs to begin to overtake my pain.

The woman could pray for me if she liked. I needed to move on to the rest of my bucket list. I finally got it. I was supposed to be a preacher. I had been given the gift. I simply decided not to embrace it. I had become my own waste of a man. This is the reason God was canceling my lifetime, and I would die today in a body of water. I did not know what God had put Dooley on this earth to do but from that standpoint, I was no better than Dooley. I simply found a different way to run from my purpose and my best self. My lack of Godly love coming here proved I was not ready to embrace my path.

Even what I was doing today may not even qualify as me being my best self because I was doing all that I was doing without fear and procrastination because the clock was ticking. It wasn't real. I was a fake. I was worse than the story of Scrooge. I still wanted to be elevated. I still wanted to be a hero. I still wanted my life to be about me even in the last hours of it. It was wrong but that was how I felt right now.

I slid down into the Rambler. I put the ice back into the sling and back into the wraps for my head. I sat in the car pondering my failures.

"Lord, I understand that you have had enough of my disobedience. I understand now that my life is not actually about me. I understand that I need to help those that are in distress and need encouragement. I'm supposed to not need to be a hero. I just need to show love...genuine love without expecting anything in return. With your help, I'm willing to do that with whatever time I have left...and maybe, maybe I can change your mind and you'll let me live past today."

I now felt bad for the words I spoke to Dooley. It was not Christ-like at all. *Vengeance is yours Lord. Please forgive me for my pride.*

I leaned back against the headrest. I had one more thing I hoped I would get to do with the last hours of my life...At least one more good thing before God takes his vengeance out on me...unless I can convince him not to.

Let me know if I'm still going to die today, Lord.

# Death Wish

I finally made it to the garage next to the building where my old friend Ricky worked. Last time I spoke with him, at the poker match where I defrauded him, he was working hard to move up in this firm. I hoped he still worked there. Rumors on the street suggested he was doing well at this same firm.

The icepacks were no longer icy. The sling helped to lessen the burden of arm on my shoulder by some small degree. The throbbing in my head diminished to a dull, yet nearly trivial pain. My ribs still hurt. I probably had some that were cracked. I expected that my death might well come before I overcome that. I took several short breaths and readied myself to exit the 1970 AMC Rambler Rebel.

Pain shot through my torso as I slid my legs out of the car for the last time. Standing was difficult, but eventually I found myself upright. I made an agreement with my legs that together we would defy the pain in the rest of my body to accomplish my few remaining tasks before God would exact his revenge on my life...if I could not convince him to change his mind.

A few more cautious, deep, painful breaths and I was relieved that my legs agreed to pick up the slack. I took one last look at the car that had taken me five years to almost finish. The body work was done. The engine was pristine, except for the non-vintage starter. The inside of the car deserved better than human touch. The only thing it needed now was some candy apple red paint and a quality clear coat. After that, Ricky could drive his car in parades and be accosted by car collectors of every age. I envied Ricky when I stole from him. I envied him still today but not for the same reasons.

The street between the garage and the office building was well shaded with mature trees. It was a sleepy little street just off a major road downtown. I took the envelope with the car title out of my back pocket just to make sure I had it. I decided to keep it in my hand.  It was the least my right hand could do protruding from a sling uselessly.

My legs carried me until I eventually entered the building. The sign inside the lobby directed me to the firm Ricky worked for.  Liston Investment Firm – Suite 901.  That was the company I remembered, and it was the only one on the board that made any sense. As I entered the elevator, I checked the time on my cell phone, which read 4:25. I had made it here in time, I hoped.

I tried to tuck in my shirt but could not reach around to the back of my right side.  It would have to do as it was.  The elevator took me to the ninth floor and was a much smoother ride than the one in the parking garage.  I felt every little bump in the descent from that one.  The office building elevator gently came to a stop for which I was grateful.  I exited the elevator into the ninth-floor lobby section.

There was a glass wall and a glass door which I opened carefully.  The door felt heavy and pain shot from the front of my body to the back.  I managed to get the door open as the woman at the front desk watched me struggle.  She was a pretty blonde and looked to be in her early twenties.  She could have been a cheerleader for a professional sports team or a model...or anything she wanted to be.  Men like to have beautiful women around in most professions regardless of their intellect or professional capacity – it's a shallow reality.

I approached the desk. "I'm here to see Ricky Watters," I explained.

"Who may I tell him is here to see him?"

"Johnny Boxton." I thought for a moment.  "Tell him I finished his car."

The woman had a puzzled look. "Just tell him.  He'll know what it means."  She seemed satisfied with the instructions.

There was an older man standing in the lobby.  He'd just finished shaking hands with a man that looked like he must have been a broker for the firm.  The old man seemed to take notice of me as though he wanted to say something to me. He didn't and I didn't care. Fewer words for me to respond to.

The receptionist pushed a few buttons, "Hello Mr. Watters. I have a Mr...Boxton at the front for you...yess sir...Boxton, sir. He says he finished your car." There was silence, "Yes. That's what he said, Sir. He finished your car." She continued now looking at me, "I'll let him know."

She pushed a button on her headset and returned her focus to me, "He said he'll be right out. You just caught him. He was about to leave." Her demeanor changed and she seemed to feel more comfortable with me being there. "Are you ok, sir? Can I get you anything? Water? Coffee? Well, we may not have coffee at this point."

"I'm fine," I said shaking my head.

I looked at one of the chairs. I wanted to sit down and lean back against the wall. The chairs looked very comfortable. I knew it would be hard to stand up again. Instead I just closed my eyes and focused on slow, careful, deep breaths.

"BANG!" A loud noise came from nearby. Some loud, unintelligible words were exchanged somewhere down the hall where I could not see. A young man taking long strides appeared from the left of the receptionist. He wore plain clothes: some holey jeans, black boots, and a fashionable, short sleeve buttoned shirt that was scarcely buttoned. He had many silver chains and more tattoos.

He glared at the receptionist, "You might have a shot at me now, babe!"

The receptionist returned a look that was fitting and expressed her disgust.

He took the stairs a short stride from the elevator doors and nearly attacked the stairway door disappearing through it.

"Crazy day, man! Whoa! What happened to you, old man?" Ricky asked, greeting me with a wide grin as he walked up to me.

He stretched his arms wide as if to hug me. I put up my left hand weakly to let him it would be too much for me.

"I was gonna ask how you been but...MAN...I can see you have had – it – rough!" He stood back taking a look at me.

"Chelsea," Ricky addressed the young lady sitting at the front desk. She turned her attention to him. "This man standing before you is the only man in the history of Kingler High school wrestling team to EVER...EVER go undefeated for two straight years. This man was a legend."

The words felt like he was talking about someone else. It had been a time long since I felt like I could do much of anything.

Ricky continued, "This man was flawless in his technique and he outlasted everybody." Ricky grinned taking in my look and his face changed, I supposed he was wondering what had happened to me to not fulfill that promise of potential. "Yup...Johnny Box...he would...Box you in and you couldn't do NUTHIN."

His face grew plain as he studied my look, "The preacher who could kick your ass. Looks like you got YOUR ass kicked right now."

I could see that he wanted to ask what happened, but he changed the subject. "Come on back, man, let's talk." He motioned me to follow him. "You finished that Rambler you stole from me at that poker match?" he said jokingly. He didn't know yet that I actually did steal it from him. I wondered how he would take the shameful news. I hoped and expected that getting it back nearly finished would be a reasonable exchange.

A young lady came walking quickly, almost trotting, from one of the offices down the hall in the direction the tattooed young man had come from. Makeup had run down her face and she was trying wipe water from her eyes. Something about her face struck me oddly and I had a strong sense of something very desperate in her face. I watched her teeter to the bathroom just around the corner from the elevators.

I could not stop watching her. Some deep sadness had been thrust upon the young woman and the look in her face stayed with me...it was a ...she was overwhelmed with emotion and she looked ready to explode.

"C'mon bro!" Ricky seemed oblivious to the girl. "She'll be ok. They blow up every other month like that. I don't know how she puts up with it though or why she hasn't been fired. She's better off without that jerk." Ricky resumed his thirty-inch stride that I had difficulty matching today.

"We never talked about what happened to your mom, man. Last time we hung out, I was drunk and running my mouth. Awful thing, bro...your mom getting sick like that just before you graduated. Man! The stuff that happens to people sometimes."

Ricky had a small office with nice wood furniture. There were two comfortable looking chairs in his office. "How's your dad?"

"I dunno," I said. "I haven't seen him in a while." "You should go see him, bro. You didn't know I actually go to his church, did you?" Ricky seemed proud of himself.

I was surprised, "To my dad's church, huh?"

Ricky's smile, which appeared cosmetically improved and was perfect, glowed. "Yeah bro. There's a service tonight. You should go."

"You going?" I asked doubtfully.

"Yeah bro. My girlfriend sings in the choir there. Cute little red head...spunky too. Smart...little young for me but she doesn't mind...I SURE don't mind."

I grinned feeling happy for Ricky. "So, you finished the car, huh?" Ricky asked.

I took a peek over my left shoulder wondering if the young lady had returned to work or would she just stay in the bathroom until time to go home.

Ricky didn't wait for me to answer, "Man that thing was a rust bucket. I had no idea what I was gonna do with it. I always wanted to get into cars, but I never got started."

"It's not completely finished," I explained. "It needs paint."

Ricky stopped to think. "Wait. You kept the car for five years. You did everything but paint it, and now you're giving it back to me." He paused pondering the situation. "I mean, I'm not complaining at all. If you got it running...man...that's a hell of a lot more than I could've done. But why give it back now? You could have given it back earlier ...or...or after it was painted. Hell, why you giving it back in the first place?"

"Had to be today," I snorted. "And I cheated."

"What? Wait...You cheated? You? At what?"

"Poker," I answered dryly, taking another look over my shoulder.

Ricky was shaking his head. "Wow...uhh, hey, why don't you sit down. Lemme help you." Ricky bounced out of his chair to stand beside me. He pulled a guest chair away from his desk, "What the...?" The chair was full of water. Ricky looked up at the ceiling. Not finding any explanation, he put his hand in the water. He shook his hand and wiped it on his pants.

"That is weird, man." He slid the chair out into the hallway and returned. "Have a ..." he was stuck in dead silence for a moment. "What the HELL? HEY, YOU GUYS PLAYING A DUMB PRANK ON ME?" Ricky was deeply annoyed, "I SIT CLIENTS IN THESE CHAIRS!"

A coworker came to Ricky's office and peeked in. "Wow. Those chairs must be SOAKING wet for all that water to sit there..."

There was a sudden, faint commotion down the hall. First, voices and then as I listened it became muffled screams. I couldn't hear anything else Ricky said. I slid the keys to Ricky's car onto the desk and the car title already signed.

"I gotta go, Rick,"

Ricky tried to split his attention between me and the chairs and the keys and his co-worker unsuccessfully. I was able to slide out of his office without any further argument. I wanted to check on the young lady and I quickly reached the lobby.

Another young lady exited the bathroom with a look of concern. She approached the girl at the front desk, "Did you see which way Allie went?" She asked the girl named Chelsea sitting at the front desk.

"She went into the stairs," answered the receptionist. "I think she just tried to come back out of the stairs, but that guy stopped her."

"She never takes the stairs," said the girl who must have been Allie's friend. "I'm gonna go down and see if I can catch her."

"It sounded like she was running up the stairs," said Chelsea returning to the phone lines. "I think they're fighting," she said softly mouthing the words then returning her attention to whomever was on the other side of her headset, "Liston Investing, how may I direct your call?"

I turned towards the stairs and a sense of dread came over me and I knew I had to act. Without even knowing why, I ran into the stairwell and up the stairs, shedding the sling as I ran. I hoped that what I was doing was totally foolish and an overreaction. The pain in my ribs and shoulder seemed to disappear and there was only a sense of dread as time slowed and the stairs flashed by.

In what seemed like an instant, I was up the stairs and bursting through a door that opened to the fading sunlight. I scanned the roof. To my right was a young lady, wearing the same clothes as the young lady with the running make-up. The tattooed man with chains had both hands clenched around her neck. He was dragging her to the edge of the roof as she struggled.

"STOP" I screamed at the tattooed man. He turned to look at me, not releasing the girl who was pulling at his wrists in futility. My legs did not wait for my mind to process what was happening. The man's face contorted as he funneled his bodily energy into his legs and shoulders to throw the woman over the edge.

I reached the edge of the building as her feet left the ground and I grabbed her waist with my left arm, twisting her away from the roof. I felt a lurch in ribs and my shoulder as I ripped the woman away from the man. His face contorted again into an image of extreme frustration.

He launched himself at me, and I turned to shield the girl with the left side of my body as I released her into my battered right arm. He swung as I raised my left shoulder and ducked my head. His punch landed squarely in my shoulder. If that's all he had, there would not be any issue disabling him.

I released the young woman and she stepped back, her hands on her throat. I positioned myself between them as the man took hold of my shirt and began pulling and twisting me to the edge of the roof.

As a trained wrestler, I was close enough to him to finish this fight already. Unfortunately, not all of my body was responding. My grip was still very strong, and I knew I could still hurt him. I pushed hard against the half-wall with my foot and grabbed him in an armpit and squeezed hard.

He winced in pain, "WHAT THE HELL KINDA GRIP IS THAT?" he cried, lurching himself away from me. Now there was space between us, and I needed to get my hands on him again to end this.

"C'mere, old man. You gonna regret XXXutting' your nose in my business!"

I stepped away from the edge of the roof as he swung wildly – as though he would knock me out with one punch. I caught his wrist in mid-air and then drove my knee into his ribs. It was a move I had practiced a lot many years ago and I didn't have to think about it. Lifting my left leg was a jarring move to me, though; I would not do that again.  The knee strike was supposed to be the first of several moves done in a sequence, instead, I would have to do something I could actually follow-through on.

He buckled only slightly and stepped back again, "Ok, Old man.  We gonna do this the hard way."

He launched into a flurry of kicks which I slid back away from waiting until just the right moment.  I just needed to get my hands on him again.  I recognized my chance as soon as he began a big kick and I lunged into his body.  I dampened the kick and slammed my head into his face.

He recoiled again, with a bloody nose – only this time, I had done too much.  The sudden move required muscles connected to my back and ribs and I now felt pain shooting through the right side of my body that did not stop shooting.  I felt waves of pain and my best hope was to get him down before he could catch on.

I tightened my right arm, folded against my body and showed him my teeth; more from the pain but maybe he'd not know the difference.  He started swinging his fists again.  His fist struck me hard on my elbow as I covered.  I felt this blow in much of my torso.  He launched again into barrage of fancy kicks that I slipped and evaded clumsily now.  The right side of my body was not keeping up with my left.

If I was I healthy and had the use of both hands, I'd have simply waited for the right moment to catch his leg in the air and then my wrestling experience would take over.  I wasn't healthy and didn't have both hands and it became quickly apparent to him.  I realized now that I was hunched over protecting my right side in an obvious way – I'd given him my secret.

I could see the look of possible defeat melt from his face now replaced by a sinister grin.  My weakness was revealed.  He launched forward again, this time focusing on my right side.

He kicked me again before I could begin moving away to lessen the blow.  This time I felt the full brunt of his kick against my arm and ribs and the right side of my body buckled and I could not stand upright anymore. The ground would have been welcome, but this would-be-murderer of the young woman chose to catch me.

He now had a half-nelson grip around my soft shoulder and my neck, and the pain was blinding.

I heard the woman scream, "STOP…PLEASE…STOP…He was just trying to help!"

I was suddenly twisted into a different position. The man freed me of the half-nelson lock and punched me hard in my ribs again. The pain was stunning. He spun me around and now his hands were hard around my throat as his foot tripped me. I landed hard on the ground; his hands still clasped around my neck. I grabbed his face with my still useful hand and still strong grip. He cried out as he yanked his head away from my grip. I had vigorously squeezed a soft place just under his jawbone and one of his hands left my throat.

It was not enough for me to get free. He was now free of my grip and he slammed my left arm to the ground and put his knee on it. He now straddled my chest and pressed my neck hard down to the rooftop gravel with both hands and I could not breathe. I could not move to stop him from killing me. His grasp around my neck made his intentions clear. He pressed both thumbs into my windpipe. I struggled with my legs to no avail. I could see a look of both hatred and satisfaction in his face – it was evil.

"Just DIE old man!" he commanded.

Why God? Why let him kill me? I thought. It was not the last thing I thought I would see today.

I thought I was going to die in water, with my lungs filling up suddenly and the last sounds being the silence of the water, a peaceful end. Instead, all I could hear was the sinister commands of this bully telling me to die. The fear I thought I was free of today was rising in my chest and bursting into my limbs. My vision became hazy and my eyes felt like they were burning.

I was suddenly released, and the man rolled off me. I could no longer hear anything but a ringing in my ears and I saw Ricky struggling with the man. The next thing I saw was Ricky's face leaning down close to mine. I saw his lips moving and eventually I could understand him screaming at me.

"JOHNNY...JOHNNY...CAN YOU HEAR ME?" he asked. I nodded.

I was being lifted now by two strong hands. Ricky pulled me up, but I wanted to lay down. I laid back down onto the gravel pulling away from my savior, reeling in pain.

Ricky was breathing deeply, "How'd you know, man?"

I pulled my heels up toward my butt gently, my knees pointing up, my eyes looking up into the sky, "I dunno, man." I coughed before I could continue. "Just something in her eyes, I guess."

Ricky kneeled beside me. The young woman was standing nearby. The only sounds now were the wind blowing through the machinery somewhere nearby, a large air conditioner unit humming and Allie's soft sobs.

I wanted to go to sleep. My head hurt again now. I coughed a bit more making my headache and pain in my ribs so much worse. My shoulder felt as if it was on fire and it hurt to breathe. My throat felt battered as well.

If I had already said something like good-bye to my father already, I would have just asked to be left here to die – staring up into the sky. It felt like freedom was just within reach. The clouds were close and slow. It was as if they called out to me.

The vision I received suggested I would die in water. The miracle this morning confirmed it. I asked God if he'd changed his mind. Then I saw water again in Ricky's chairs. I accepted my fate and I felt as if there was not much more I could do. I no longer wanted to be a hero but now I was one. I didn't feel any different. I didn't feel like someone whose name was going to be on a wall or whose face would be molded in bronze or stone. I felt like a man in pain who was spent and who almost got choked to death on a hot roof. That's what I was – spent and beaten.

Ricky stood up. "Come on, hero," he said. I shook my head to be left alone.
"You sure?"
I nodded, trying not to move my body too much.
"Nope!" Ricky insisted. "I'm not leaving you up here. Come on."

Ricky was gentle and yet strong. It was as if all the years that passed since we wrestled passed more quickly for me than for him.
With much straining and gnashing of teeth, I finally made it to my feet.
The young woman left the arms of her coworker and gently came to hug me. She stared into my eyes but didn't seem able to talk. She kissed me on the cheek and her friend helped her to walk through the door in the middle of the roof.
Ricky and I watched them go as I lumbered toward the door. We made it into the stairwell and the stairs seemed to be a very long way down.

Ricky saw the way I studied them, "Sorry, bro. You gotta go down at least one flight before we can catch the elevator."
I smiled, trying to make light of it.
"I'll go down first. Put your hand on my shoulder. I got you," Ricky instructed.

Ricky positioned himself on the step below and in front of me. As I stepped down, he stepped down, both of us holding onto the left railing. I remembered that Ricky was a good friend in high school. He had returned to town to find work near his family. He'd had enough of living up north in the cold. He had been drinking too much and talking too much about all his financial achievements and the women he was dating.

I was jealous of the life Ricky was living and something ugly came over me when I saw that he was winning at poker. It was something bitter and resentful in me that said NO MORE. He'd just purchased a car. I had no money to buy a car in any shape. He'd found a real steal on something that was going to be worth a lot once it was restored. He didn't have the skills to restore the car and I did. So, I rationalized it a thousand different ways. He could afford to get another. He deserved to lose his money gambling so foolishly. Why do people like me always seem to get the worst luck despite always trying to do what was right?

I realized that was a key moment in my life. It was the first moment in my life that I ever admitted defeat—that I ever admitted I was not man enough or secure enough ...or good enough to earn it...to earn my own success. That was the moment I became a failure in life. Before that moment, I always fought the good fight. I always got back up. I always found a way to smile no matter how much life hurt.

Life...God...took my mother while I was young. It nearly destroyed my father. We didn't have great insurance and cancer was expensive. My mother didn't get the best care. My parents turned to God and he apparently declined to help my mother. Then my wife and I lost our son. My preaching days had been over but after my son was taken, I didn't want to serve God, talk to God or hear from Him.

How was I supposed to help people give their lives to a God that had already taken so much from me. Why do some people have everything just go their way? Why did I always have to work so hard for every – single –thing? I didn't care about getting back up anymore. I didn't care about being tough enough for whatever happened next; not anymore. Why should I bother?

I stopped. I stood standing on the stairs looking down at the remaining steps until the next landing.

"I got it," I said. I realized the answer to the question was, *Because I was made to*, I thought. Not everyone can handle what I've had to handle, I suppose. Life had thrown all kinds of evil twists at me and I was still here. Today, I have even done some good in this world.

Ricky turned to look at me to ensure I was ok. I did not want to look him in the eyes, "GO RICK! I'm FINE." I would not grunt or grimace anymore. I was made to endure suffering and that is what I will do today, for however much more time my today lasts. I thought to myself about a poem I once read by William Ernest Henley. Part of the poem seemed to be the unconscious goal of my life.

"...In the fell clutch of circumstance
I have not winced nor cried aloud.
Under the bludgeonings of chance
My head is bloody, but unbowed...."

*I will not wince nor cry aloud*, I said to myself silently with my lips as I steeled myself to continue down the stairs unaided. I focused on breathing and just taking one step at a time until I finally emerged into the air-conditioned air in the office hallway. Ricky led me around the corner, and I heard him hit the button on the wall. The elevator came quickly, and I stepped inside as Ricky held the doors ajar.

"I can't believe you saved her, man? You're all busted up. I don't know what happened to you before you came here but you are busted up good, man." Ricky asked.

I looked up to the elevator ceiling, "It had to be done. Might as well have been me."
Ricky looked at me as if he wanted to say something.

"What?" I demanded.

Ricky shook his head before relenting, "Man, I always admired you. I don't know how you took so much shit from life and always kept getting up. You always had enough left over to help someone else."

"You remember Debbie...that runs that diner?" Rick asked.

"Sure," I said bracing myself for the next bump in the elevator ride down.

"She told me the story how you helped her sister."

"What?" I had no idea what Ricky was talking about.

"You remember we had to run every day for practice. There was that one day, we were just starting back for the new season training...everybody was gassed. We were like done. There was this girl, I think she was on the track team. She was sitting down crying beside the path. Everyone was so tired. We all just passed her by. You carried her back to the field."

"I don't remember that," I said.

"Well, you did." Ricky said. "That was Debbie's little sister. She sprained her ankle in that big hole by the leaning post."

It was starting to come back to me. "Oh ok. All I wanted to do was take a nap after that man."

"Yeah. I think everybody on the team slept early that night. Most of us were late to school the next day too," Ricky explained.

"You always keep going man. I don't know how you go through all you go through and you still keep doing...keep doing for others, bro."

I appreciated his words, but they only made the admission I had shared even worse. Here it comes. I could see the puzzled look on his face.

"So, you said you cheated ...at poker?" Rick asked.
I nodded gently, trying to ignore pain coming from many places. "Yup."

"Why?" Ricky said, shaking his head.

"I guess I was jealous of you," I answered.

The elevator slowed gently and came to a stop. The door opened. Allie was standing in the middle of the lobby with her friend draped around her shoulders.

She smiled at me through her tears and blurred makeup. "I didn't say thank you. You saved my life." I nodded. I was expecting to simply smile and wait until the elevator doors closed to continue on my journey.

"Don't go yet, man. Let her say her peace." Rick insisted.

I stepped out of the elevator feeling a bit dizzy. Throwing up would be a miserable pain right now. I decided now was a good time to sit down anyway. I made my way to the lobby chairs and was relieved to see that the chairs were not full of water.

I sat carefully, "Can I get some water?"

"Of course," answered Rick. "Be right back."

Ricky disappeared around the corner behind the main desk wall. The chair was a relief. I lay my head back against the wall taking measured breaths. The old man was still in the lobby now taking in everything from his own chair on the opposite side of the lobby.

Allie spoke something to her friend who smiled and left the room. Allie came to sit beside me. She mirrored my pose leaning her head back against the wall. She looked over to me. I looked over to her my head still against the wall behind me. She didn't seem to know what to say so I started talking, my face now to the ceiling, my eyes closed.

"Today, I went to give a guy back his jacket. I had the jacket for months. I had no idea he thought I ruined his life. It was just a stupid misunderstanding, but you know what...he got fired from a job he HATED. He got broke up from a relationship with a girl that was horrible to him...thinking I was the cause. But...I think probably I got him a job that he would actually like... a lot. He also learned how bad that girl was to him and I got to tell him today...how much I love him...like a real friend."

I looked over to her again, "Maybe that guy doesn't really love you. But other people do. You just gotta figure out ...how to love yourself first. Then you'll see how much you have to give...how much good you can do in the world." The chair was starting to feel like it would make it difficult for me to get up. I could sleep right here.

I continued more to stay awake than to offer any real wisdom, of which I had little, "Maybe it feels like everything is shit. It doesn't have to stay that way. You can change it...one new choice at a time. Suppose you tried to do one thing different...make one thing better...what's the worst that can happen?"

Rick returned with a cold bottle of water. "Man, I got you a cold one. The front was stacked up with ones just put in."

He twisted the top off and handed it to me. I put the bottle to my lips, and it seemed to nearly flow continuously down my throat and filled a hole someplace I didn't know existed.

I positioned my hands to lift myself from the chair. I looked over to the girl, "Go do something new – create something, even something small... something you can see."

She grabbed my hand as I stared down into her teary eyes, "I ...I didn't have a father. All men want something ...something in return. You don't."

It hurt worse to partially stand than to stand all the way. "Today was my day to give," I said not looking at her.

Rick took the title from his pocket. "So... you're just giving the car back?"

I took a breath, "Yup. I loved working on that car. I got to make something ugly become beautiful. That's enough for me." I took my measured steps toward the elevator, "Good-bye, Ricky."

I knew I would never see him again. I think my tone said it. Ricky didn't reply. He just stood watching me as though he needed time to process all he'd seen and heard.

I pushed the button on the wall to call the elevator. I still had enough money in my pocket to get a one-way trip to my father's house. I wasn't sure if I would get see my wife, ex-wife or not. My mother's car was probably still available. I was sure my father kept it running but likely never drove it. I imagined it sitting in the garage like it was going to be driven the next morning by a slender brunette, about age thirty-seven. I was sure my father had the same idea.

The door to the elevator was about to close, but just then the end of a cane slipped between the doors. The elevator doors opened revealing the old man from the lobby. "Hope you don't mind a straggler," he entered the elevator. I nodded and the man stepped on as though he assumed I would not object.

The elevator began moving. The floor numbers changed from nine to eight, then from eight to seven. The man spoke, "That Rambler in the parking garage is the one you just finished working on?"

I smiled and nodded. "That's the one."

The old man nodded. "I saw it in the parking lot. I had to come back inside to get my cell phone. I was thinking about that Rambler the whole time." He paused before continuing as I stood in silence. "It runs clean?" he asked.

"Purrs...idling and flat out." It felt good to describe it that way. "Not mine to sell though."

The old man held up his hand, "Oh no...that's not what I was thinking."

The elevator now showed floor three.

"I have been in the car repair business for forty-five years but...it's time for me to think about retiring." He nodded gently forming his next words, "My son died in Iraq. My wife...my wife could care less about cars and...well...she wants to travel."

I wondered why he was telling me all of this.

He made a big sigh, "I don't have any grands to take it on and my family doesn't know anything about cars." The old man came to stand in front of me to command my full attention.

"Where did you learn about cars from?" he asked.

I squinted, wondering why it mattered to him.

"Jimbo's...mostly."

The old man smiled, "I know him. I know him well. I...I don't have the clientele he has...don't want it but... I know his work." He put his thumb to his chin. "How would you like to run my shop for me...run my family's business? I can't bear to sell it but I'm too old to run it. I need someone that loves cars as much as me...and that I can trust."

"You own that shop on Main? I asked.

"Yes. Plus the one up north on State road forty-five and another shop in Maitland," he explained.

I couldn't remember the name of his shop, but I now knew who he was.

I stopped leaning against the wall and stared him square in the eyes scanning them. He was serious.

"Mr...Davis...I think it is. I'm flattered. Any other day, I would have said yes without a second thought."

I didn't realize he didn't have anyone to pass his shop on to. His shops had a good reputation with American cars and a couple mainstream foreign brands. It was a very successful, but much less adventurous enterprise. I liked the interesting cars and interesting problems I got to work on in Jimbo's shop, but it was mostly a waiting game. Also, the clientele could be scary if Jimbo didn't keep me separate from that part of the business.

The Davis shops would be a steady flow of, mostly, less interesting challenges but it would be stable. Soccer moms in Volvos and businessmen in Mercedes Benzes that tried to sound knowledgeable about cars would be an easy job. If I were going to be alive tomorrow, it would be appealing. I was a bit saddened thinking that this opportunity should have come a few days ago.

"Today is too late. I am...outta time," I said without explaining.

The man gave me a curious look, "I'm not sure I understand, but here's my number anyway."

He gave me his business card. "If things change, give me a call...won't you?" he asked.

I nodded, "Sure." I was thinking how funny it is that things work out a certain way. I slid his business card into my pocket, thinking how awful it would be to die with a ticket to a new life in my possession.

The floor number changed to one. The elevator gently slowed to a stop. I still felt it. I refused to make any sounds, but I am sure my face reflected some pain.

"I do hope you can rest and heal," he said as he turned to exit the elevator.

I let him walk out before me, as much to be courteous as to not be seen struggling.

He turned back to me as he exited the elevator, "Just so you know. My offer is serious."

I smiled and nodded.

He exited the downstairs lobby door and with a short walk he stood beside a four-door model Excalibur. I thought it might be a mid-1980s model. I had a toy one in the box I gave to my wife's nephew. The car had a lot of detail, and I always wanted to restore one. I couldn't see the front at all and very little of the back so I couldn't tell which model it was. I didn't want to know. Knowing would only bring me pain.

I sat on a bench, pulling out my cell phone. I estimated that I had just enough for a taxi to a bus stop a little way from my father's house. As I was near downtown, and it wasn't late yet, there were still plenty of taxis about. An Uber would have been cheaper, but I didn't have a credit card. The dispatch told me there was a car nearby. I would have a ride in a few minutes. I didn't see any water anywhere, and the only water I would expect to see at any point in the rest of my day would be the lake near my dad's house. I prayed I had changed God's mind. If not, the lake would somehow be my death after all. I would know very soon.

# All This Time

A yellow Crown Victoria pulled alongside the curb in front of me. It had only been a few minutes wait, but my muscles and joints had continued to stiffen. The driver got out and came around to the other side of the car. He scanned the sidewalk, apparently looking for the person that called him. I raised my left hand and he returned a smile at first. His face then contorted to indicate his concern over the way I looked.

I stood, still holding a promise to myself that I would not wince...or at least not cry aloud. Instead, I measured my breaths and trusted my legs to carry the slack. The driver opened the back door and reached towards me to offer help.

"I'm good," I said waving him off. He nodded, smiling through his look of concern.

I was glad that he closed the door though. Having to trust my right arm to pull the door closed would have been more interesting than I wanted to test. I buckled my seat belt and leaned into the corner made by the door and the back-seat bench.

The driver slid in and closed his door, "Rough day, huh?" I didn't respond. "Where to, buddy?" the driver asked.

"Corner of Slaten and Conway," I said.

That was a bus stop not far from my parents' house which was in a sleepy little neighborhood near a lake east of downtown. My father's church was even farther east. I had decided to take a chance that my father would still be at home. If not, at least my mother's car would be there, and I could borrow it to drive to the church.

My mother would have wanted me to go to church on day like this, knowing it would be my last – maybe. But more than anything, I wanted to see Mom. That house was the closest thing. I also didn't have enough cab fare to get all the way to the church. As the taxi driver left downtown, he climbed onto the expressway.

"Why didn't you just ride Anderson all the way out?" I asked. Anderson was a long one-way street that ended at Lake Underhill road which went around Lake Underhill and passed Conway which led to my father's neighborhood. It was too late now. We were going to go over Lake Underhill on the expressway.

"It's faster, man. There's too much traffic on Anderson this time of the day," the taxi driver explained.

It was too late to argue. The next exit was on the other side of the lake. I now sat erect, watching the cars passing by and being passed by the taxi. The driver entered the flow of traffic which was heavy but still fast. As the road inclined to cross over the lake, the taxi driver came alongside a semi to the right side of it— the side where the trucks have the worst visibility–the suicide side. Almost as if on cue, the truck swerved into our lane responding to another driver's attempt to zip into a lane.

The truck was now coming at us in slow motion. The taxi driver responded by swerving into the next lane. The driver honked his horn rudely. The taxi continued on and eventually exited the expressway onto Conroy and eased up to the traffic light to cross Lake Underhill road which was fed by Anderson.

My nerves took ease that we had made it past a possible culmination of my morning vision, the miracle of the water in the bed and the miracle of the water in the chairs – all prophesying my death by drowning. The driver had no idea of the anxiety that had just coursed through my nerves. The tension now leaving my body seemed to take energy with it as well. I just wanted to get out of his car and put my feet on the ground. I told him which bus stop I wanted to get to. I let it slip that the bus stop would not be far from my father's house.

"How far you have to ride the bus?" he asked.

"About two miles," I answered. "I'm already close to my mark on the meter. I'll just get a bus going south," I explained.

"Man, I gotta go south anyway to get back to the airport. I was just uptown for a bit. If your father is off South Conway, just give me the address. I will turn the meter off at twenty," he offered.

I laid my head back into the seat. "Thanks."

"Yeah, man. You in no condition to stand there at a bus stop or climbing onto a bus. I'm gonna pass right by where you gotta go."

I still wanted to get out of his car, but I was relieved I would not have to stand at the bus stop. We soon passed the bus stop where I was planning to wait, and I saw people...standing. I directed the driver on which street to turn onto, challenging him to ignore the directions coming from his GPS.

The taxi finally pulled alongside the driveway of my father's house—the house my mom used to live in. It was the house I finally ran from to escape all the bad memories which seemed to blot out all the good ones from so long ago. The back of his small truck was opened. It had a camper top and both the tailgate and the back of the camper were open revealing bags at inside the back of the truck. I owed the driver $19.75. I gave him the rest of my money and got out of the car carefully.

My father appeared from inside the garage. "GOOD LORD!" he cried out as he saw me, rushing to put another set of bags in the back of his truck. "My Son!" He rushed to me, carefully wrapping his arms around me. "What in the world happened to you, Johnny?" he asked taking a look at me, still embracing me.

"Long day, dad." I didn't really want to explain it all. I just wanted to sit down in a comfortable chair. If I was alive tomorrow, I would be glad to explain it then. I waved good-bye to the taxi driver.

I refused Dad's help walking to the house, still trying to execute on my pride.  Dad followed me closely, nevertheless, watching every step I made.

As I reached the front of Dad's truck, I saw a canvas covering, what looked to be, a car.  "Does it still run?" I asked gazing at the canvas.

"It did last time I took it out.  Probably needs a battery now."  A faint smile appeared on Dad's face, "I always wondered if that time you spent with your Granddad working on that thing is what got you into cars; God rest his soul."

"I'm glad you saved it," I said turning to enter the house.

"Your mother made sure I left that for just you and your grandfather to ...to bond with.  I never had any interest anyway."  Dad stroked the canvas and patted his knuckle on the car then opened the door to the house.

I knew that me working on her car with Grandpa made her happy.  Maybe that's why I chose to fix cars for a living after she left us.  I wanted to take the canvas off, but I also didn't.  Looking at the shape of mom's car made me glad and sad at the same time.

Dad stepped up into the house and turned to me, "I made some Texas Hash earlier.  Are you hungry? I was about to head out to the church, but you're welcome to stay...or come with me."

I strained, stepping up into the house from the garage floor.  "Sure," I answered.

I didn't really want to go with him, but I did want something to eat. Texas Hash was a rice casserole type of dish that my mother must have taught him to make. If it was anything like what mom used to make, I would take some.

My father looked me over inside the house, "Why don't cha...go and clean yourself up." He studied me a bit longer. "Looks like you're almost my size now," he said with a smirk. "You can help yourself to any of my shirts. My pants aren't gonna fit you yet though." I'll heat you up some food."

He paused before turning to head into the kitchen. "It's good to have you home."

I nodded in thought. I wanted to still be angry with my father for betraying my mother during her illness. I didn't give my own feelings much thought other than I knew I wanted to be here before I died. I wanted to see my mother...or the place where she lived. It seemed like I should have a chance to say good-bye to her...or see you soon...or something. I wanted to see my father too...just not for the same reasons or reasons that I really understood.

I went to the bathroom just down the hall away from the main room and turned on the hot water. I must have grown since I was last here. I didn't remember the bathroom counter being so far away, so low to me. My father kept the small bathroom clean. It didn't seem as though anyone else lived in the house. I was relieved that my father hadn't filled some void in his life with some woman not my mother. Maybe it was selfish of me to not want him moving on but that was how I felt. I wanted to be as close to mom as I could be right now and seeing her things in the house gave me some peace.

There was a radio somewhere in the back of the house playing a jazz radio station. I ran the hot water and stared at myself in the long mirror. He added some fancy lights above the mirror give me a well-lit view of myself. I looked very much like I had been dragged in from the outside by a cat or a dog. My face was a bit swollen and my bottom lip was split. I had knots on both sides of my face from where Elliot had taken his frustration out on me and the cut from the Italian guy's expensive shoe was puffy now. My hair was a mess and there was a bit of blood on my shirt. There were faint finger marks on both sides of my neck. Other than that, I was just a bit wrinkled. I suppose that was from having dried out in odd fashion from nearly being drowned in a bathtub. I could probably have used a fresh shirt, but I didn't want to go through what my right shoulder would likely take me through.

I ran the hot water over my hands for a bit and then washed them. The hot water gave me a sensation of being relaxed that

I hadn't felt all day. My tense, spasmic muscles released in my arms, shoulders, and part of my back and some of the pain I felt melted down to more tolerable levels.

I found a towel under the counter neatly folded in a stack of neatly folded towels. They were perfectly stacked. The cleaning products under the counter and extra toothbrushes and unopened boxes of toothpaste all looked like my father had become a bit of a neat freak.

My mother was the one that always demanded we both clean up after ourselves and then after we made attempts to do so, she'd clean up after us anyway. Everything she cleaned or arranged always looked so much better after she did it. There was fresh potpourri on the counter, a bowl of mints and a ceramic seagull. There was a painting of a huge wave on the wall opposite the sink. My mother used to love the beach and we spent many early Saturday mornings at one when I was young.

My father appeared at the open doorway to the bathroom with a couple of shirts in his hands, "These are a little tight for me around the middle, but they're new. I liked the way they looked in some online pictures. Of course, when they got here, and I tried to squeeze into 'em...I don't have that shape anymore. Probably look great on you though," Dad suggested with a look of satisfaction.

I couldn't tell him they would be wasted on me. I smiled and continued looking at the picture of the waves which had brought back memories for me, "Dad," I called his attention. "Do you remember learning to surf and trying to teach me?"

"Sure do! You picked it up a lot faster than I thought you would," he exclaimed.

"Do you remember us getting pulled into a rip current? You helped me break free, but you got dragged out. Mom and I...thought we lost you. People around us were all freaking out. Lifeguards were coming from everywhere!" Dad became silent in thought.

I sighed trying to recall more details, "You ended up down the beach. I can remember mom looking down the beach with her hand shadowing out the sun and staring off into the distance. Then, there was this... huge sigh of relief in her voice...she tried to sound calm like everything was just like she expected."

He nodded and then spoke, "When I saw your little shape next to your mom down the beach – I was ...beyond relieved. That hat she wore and that...that wrap she had on, flapping in the wind...I could have cried." Dad smiled, "You were trying to be calm like your mother, but your eyes were all red. I knew you'd been crying – my tough young man."

I remembered dad kneeling down, "You asked me if I was ok. You stared at me for a long time...and then it just seemed like we started packing up. Everybody on the beach started clapping and then we left."

I thought more about that day, "Mom was...she was silent in the car...it seems like the rest of the day." Dad just nodded studying my face.

"I think...before that...you guys used to be happy. You and Mom didn't talk on the way home that day." I thought more about that memory, "We never went back to the beach, did we?" Dad shook his head gently. His eyes fell towards the floor and he returned to rubbing his lips slowly.

"Your mother and I kind of...understood each other's feelings about the beach...while you were young," Dad explained.

I took a deep breath, "It seemed like everything was different after that."

"Yeah," Dad agreed. "That day changed a few things," he said. He tapped on the door frame, "I'll let you get dressed. The shirts are yours...if you want them." He put the shirts on the bathroom counter near the doorway and disappeared.

That year for my birthday, Dad got me a little used motor bike. My mother didn't say a word the rest of that day. The next day my father told me something was wrong with it and he needed to get it fixed. I never saw that bike again.

My parents weren't much fun to be around anymore after that. I used to say I missed surfing, but I think, more than anything, I missed being in a family that wasn't so afraid of what could go wrong.

I dried my hands and tucked in my shirt again where I could. I came out of the bathroom and noticed my father's awards and plaques of recognition that had been on the hallway wall were replaced by pictures of our family. I studied the pictures. There were pictures of my grandparents, long gone now, and pictures of my mother and father together. There was an old picture of me sitting on a horse holding a guitar wearing a red hat and also shots of me with my wrestling team.

There were also pictures of my mother around the time she started to get sick. I remember my mother refusing to be in pictures after she got very sick. A lump formed in my throat as I stared into the frame of the next picture. My mother took a picture with my father and some friends of the family. She was dressed kind of nice and wearing makeup and everyone was smiling but my parents; they showed their teeth but neither of them really smiled. It wasn't a happy picture and I didn't want to see any more pictures of my mother that didn't look like the woman I remembered most.

There was a painting on the wall that I didn't remember having been framed that Mom had painted. The frame made the painting look professional. There was another, smaller one near the room mom painted in. I walked into the room where she spent a lot of her time; throwing pottery and painting, when she felt well enough to be out of the bed.

My father had nearly enshrined the room. Paintings that were only canvased before now had wood backs. Ceramics Mom made were in a glass case like trophies.

There was a small, electric piano against one of the walls with some equipment. "You finally started playing piano?" I yelled out to dad.

He came into the room a few seconds later, "Yeah…had to do something in with this room when I finished displaying all your mom's stuff."

My emotions swirled and I had to take in the moment. All these years and all this time, I only really knew of the betrayal. To see that my mother had been honored in such a way was something else I needed to see before I died. This was even better than cranking up the Rambler today. I choked back tears…tears of a deep, profound satisfaction.

I changed the tone of the mood, "You gonna sell 'em?" I asked.

Dad took a deep breath, "You know…sometimes…I think…it's wrong of me not to share your mother's work with the world. She actually became quite good before… Well, I guess one day I'll be ready to – just not yet." He didn't have to finish; I think I understood.

I remembered my mother's face the day she died. She was in so much pain, but she smiled whenever I came into the room. Dad came to stand just inside the room near me silently. I could have thanked my father for letting this house still feel and look like Mom's house; her memory was still honored here.

"Dad, I'm sorry for how I talked to you that day…that day all those doctors came in," I said.

"Son, you do NOT have to apologize for how you felt that day," my father reassured me, but I needed to explain.

"Dad, I was angry with those doctors for what they said. I was angry with you because you let them keep talking – you didn't tell them to keep trying." My eyes got watery, "But …I understand now."

My dad nodded, "I understand son. Your mother…she was my best friend…for a while…my only friend." He stopped to breathe and put his hand on my shoulder, "I hope you know she found peace before she … before she went to be with the Lord."

"Yeah, I know," I said. "I saw it in her face...she couldn't even really talk but she said it with her eyes." I was starting to cry.

"Dad, she smiled at me...that last morning...she forced the words...she said, 'I'm ready, Son. Let Me Go.'

But...but I couldn't, Dad. I told her *NO*...I said *NO*, Dad...but she left anyway." Tears flooded my eyes. "She was my best friend too, Dad."

Tears flowed down my father's face. "I'm so sorry, Son. I guess...I guess I was overwhelmed. I didn't know how to say anything or how to do anything to make it any better for...for you or for me." He shook his head, "I wasn't there son...when you needed me...and I couldn't be...I didn't know how to."

"So, you...you found that woman," I reminded him.

"Yes," Dad admitted. "I thought she was helping me but...she wasn't. It only made me feel worse." It was an old, unfinished conversation that would not suddenly be finished because I might die today.

*That doesn't make it ok,* I thought. I wanted to forgive my father for that, today especially. I know mom would have wanted that. Even I wanted to finally be free of it, but I couldn't bring myself to make the words. I wiped my face and then I turned to walk away. I went to the kitchen through the great room. There were blinds covering a glass sliding door that never used to be covered. My eyes caught a glimpse of something unfamiliar through the kitchen window which overlooked the backyard. There was a covered patio now. I went to the blinds covering the sliding door and pulled the string to open the blinds as dad passed behind me going into the kitchen. "You put a pool in?" I said in surprise.

"Yep... finally got that pool I always talked about getting," said my father over the sounds of a metal spoon hitting a glass dish. "Got some grilled asparagus here, and I'll get you some iced tea too. I'll put your plate in the microwave."

I heard glass or ceramic clinking together and then I heard the gentle hum of his microwave. "If I knew you were coming, I could have grilled you some spicy pork tenderloin." The tenderloin used to be a favorite of mine...it was until I had to cook it for myself.

I was still staring out at the pool. A sinking feeling hit me in the stomach. Was I somehow going to die here...at my father's house? If that was to be my end, it seemed a cruel joke. There was nothing about dying as a hero that would come from drowning in a pool in a back yard.

Dad pulled out some silverware and set them on the table, "I gotta head out to the church in a few. You know you're welcome to stay...get in the pool if you like," my father suggested. I wanted to shout *NO*!

"I'll come with you," I blurted marching into the kitchen. I went to stand near the microwave, "Can I eat this on the way?"

"Ahhh, sure...sure," Dad answered dryly. "It would be great to see you at church." He put the food away restoring the pristine state of his, my mother's kitchen. That's what it looked like, like my mother's kitchen.

"Hey, did you send a young man to the church today?" Dad asked.

"Yup," I answered. "You able to help him?" I asked.

Dad was shuffling something noisily in the kitchen. "We did. I had the staff make a few calls to a neighborhood center, and I think we were able to get him what he needed. I told him we could help him more if came to church tonight. I told him, I believed God had a special message for him tonight."

I went to the kitchen to where Dad was standing. "I got you something...well, been waiting to give you something," my father said nervously. "I'll be right back." He disappeared into a back room.

The microwave gave a short chirp to let me know it was done. I took the plate from the microwave and then got a fork from a drawer. The drawer was neat and clean. I remember the drawer being a bit of a mess but, now this drawer was orderly. He returned quickly, "Here, this is for you." He held out a gold ring.

"What's this?" I asked.

Dad's face was contorted like he was restraining a smile, "If you want it, it's yours. I just want you to know...that...that you are always welcome...home." He nodded choking back tears, "You're my son and I love you...and...I missed you."

I took the ring from his hand, studying it. "I ...I think ...I don't think I have much time." I gave him back the ring.

"What do you mean?" my father asked.

I grabbed the glass of iced tea, "What time do your services start? Do you need to get dressed?" I asked.

"Dressed? Oh, well I just put on a jacket from my office. Service starts at 7:00 and I normally walk in about 7:30." He stood staring at me with a look of concern. "Son, what's going on? What you do mean you don't have time?" He nervously put the ring into a small box and back into his pocket.

"I know you don't want to talk about it but, those wounds look fresh, son. You in any kinda trouble?"

I smiled, "Dad, I'm...well...it's complicated."

"Is there anything I can do to help you?" my father asked.

"It's not wrestling, Dad. You can't help me with this one," I explained. My father had studied Brazilian Jiu Jitsu for years and that came in handy when I started wrestling, in an odd sort of way. But now God Himself threatened to end my life and martial arts training wouldn't help me today.

"Son..." he tried to reason with me to give him more information.

I held up my hand, "Dad, can we just go to church right now? Maybe we can talk about it tomorrow."

He took a long deep, breath. "Ok, Son."
I know he would do just about anything to help me do what I was trying to do. At this moment, I didn't have any goals...other

than to stay alive...if I could. I thought about the pool in the back yard and the prophecy of my death.

"Okay," he continued. "It'll be good to have you at church," he said, still holding a smile that was escaping his cheek muscles' grips. He didn't care what state I was in. He was just glad I was home. I knew the story of the prodigal son. That was the message of the ring. I wanted to lie down on a reclining chair beside the pool and sleep through the night. I would even be fine listening to Dad's jazz radio. The house was peaceful, as if my mother's energy seeped into the very walls, floors, and air of the house.

The house felt like...like her... how she was before that day on the beach and that look of peace on her face at the end. I wanted to bask in that energy; it was like a set of ethereal fingers combing through my hair as a soft voice sang a lull-a-bye.

But it was time to go...anywhere not near a body of water. I learned today that a bathtub was enough to be the end of me. A pool was more than enough. I carried my plate and my glass following my father out to his truck. I noticed that he didn't lock any doors or turn on any alarm.

"Pop, don't you use locks or alarms?"
My father, ever the pragmatic one, gave me a blast of wisdom, "For what? What do I have worth taking that can actually be taken from me?" He paused putting the last bag of something in the back of the truck. "Pictures? Forks and knives? Radio? Televisions? Bibles? I don't carry any pride in any of those things that I don't already have in my heart. I have peace son because I don't have a need for anything in particular. Oh, I need shelter, food, and so on – but need for stuff? Nah."

At this moment I understood exactly what he meant. Had he told me this yesterday or certainly some years back I would have thought he was losing his mind. But at this moment, it made perfect sense to me. Earlier today, I felt free. I had even accepted the possibility... the likelihood...of my death today. I only wanted a good death. I wanted a chance to make my death mean something...make my life mean something. I didn't need the car. I didn't need a fancy leather jacket. I didn't need a certain income or social status. Not needing those things was real freedom. Financial freedom seems like a nice idea until it comes with the need to own things or be able to acquire new things or a need to have the money in the first place. Being focused on giving, as I did today, instead of receiving was a type of deliverance.

"I think I understand, dad."
He cocked his head studying me in surprise. "You do, don't you," he said standing on the other side of the truck from me. He nodded and slid into the truck. "That kind of freedom...is like...an awakening, Son. It's rare. You've always been blessed...and burdened...but blessed. But this ...understanding...it opens a whole new world to you, Son."

I turned to the window. Fine day to come to my end, I thought. I put some of the Texas hash to my lips. It was good. It was better than good. It was last meal good. The little sweet roll and grilled asparagus were nearly as good. The sweet tea was beyond refreshing. It seemed to pour happiness inside of me.

My father giggled in satisfaction watching me eat as he drove along. I wiped my plate with the roll and put my nearly polished plate on the dashboard. "Been a while since you had a good meal, son?"

"I ate at Debbie's this morning," I answered.

"Good," was all he said.

"Dad, you mind if I take a short nap? Been a long day."

"Not at all, son."

I knew he wanted to talk but there wasn't any point. I came to visit him before, possibly, I died. I had come close to death a few times today and yet here I am. I hoped I would still be standing tomorrow and beyond, but this morning's prophecy was clear and had been reinforced.

I never told my father that I forgave him, but I didn't want to. I don't know why. I laid the seat back a bit and found a spot that didn't agitate my shoulder and made breathing more reasonable. I was expecting to get to the church and spend most of the rest of the night there. Perhaps I had a chance to survive the day. A few more hours and it would look like God changed his mind. I began to feel at ease.

The windshield began to show little sprinkles of gentle rain. My father turned on the windshield wipers which waved smoothly back and forth. The soft slow sound of the wipers going back and forth was soothing and my eyes grew heavy. They seemed to hold the image of the mattress full of water from this morning. I forced my mind to dismiss that thought and just focused on the blackness, the wipers, my breathing and peace.

# Water, Water, Everywhere

I woke to the sound of a car door opening and closing. I looked up and roused to consciousness just in time to see the back of my father running away from the car. I sat up and watched to see where he was running to after looking around a bit. There was an accident up ahead. Cars around Dad's truck were all stopped. I could not tell exactly what had happened or why my father felt like he needed to help. I then realized that there was a car turned the wrong way on the bridge we were on. The rain had stopped but everything was wet.

My stomach dropped. We were on a bridge. *Why are we on a bridge?* I thought. I looked around more. I recognized the water. It had to be Lake Jessup. We were nearly in the middle of the long bridge crossing Lake Jessup. "SHIT!" I said without meaning to. This must be the prophecy. Dozens of questions hit my mind. Was the bridge going to collapse under me in the car? Was another car going to slam into this car and push me over the edge? I suddenly heard a small, inaudible voice say, *Peace.* The voice was clear in my head and that voice was not mine. "I must be going crazy", I mumbled nervously.

So, I was just supposed to have peace? Knowing that this was likely how I was going to die? I took another breath. *You said you wanted to die a hero. So, go be a hero*, I reminded myself.

I got out of the car. My right shoulder felt like it was swollen nearly into a frozen position. My face was sore. The pain from my ribs hurt through to my back

Ricky said he admired my ability to keep going, I always had more in the tank. That's me—always able to do a little more. Well, that's how I am going to go. With a restrained grunt, I got out of the car. At first, I limped from the pain in my ribs but was eventually able to perform a slight trot. As I reached the front of an SUV in front of dad's truck, I could see how bad it really was.

There was a car flipped over, upside down. There was a strip of outer barrier missing on the right side of the road and a tractor-trailer just past it with a set of blown tires on the back, right side.

My father was trying to help people in the car who were upside down. I got close enough to see more detail. My father had just managed to get the car keys and placed them inside the car. Then he tried to wake the person in the car hanging upside down. He and another man tried to open the door of the car. With some effort, it finally opened. There was blood on her face and in the woman's hair. She finally responded to my father and immediately turned her attention to the back seat, screaming. Another man came around holding a young child. I could see the relief in her face seeing the child was ok.

I got within earshot of what was happening. The car turned the wrong way was empty. The tractor trailer's driver had also abandoned his seat. A young woman got out of her car and came to help. She took the small child from the man holding her. The small child seemed much more comfortable with the woman but seemed intent on focusing on her mother's welfare who was still in the upside-down car. After talking with the woman and ensuring she didn't have any neck spinal damage, my father was given a knife. The large man, likely the truck driver, got into the back seat of the car and held the woman's shoulders from behind. My father cut the woman's seat belt and they gently helped her to get down and then out of the car. The child was scrambling to get down and to be held by her mother. The mother was busy adjusting to no longer being upside down. She looked dizzy and my father held her up. That didn't stop her from picking up the small child. She slid down to the ground, still holding the child, with my father's help.

From what I could see, the woman was the worst off from the calamity. Now, there came the sound of sirens as a set of ambulances and fire trucks came towards us on the bridge, working through traffic. I stood taking in the scene. I realized now that we were on the northbound side of the bridge. It seemed so strange to see that there was not a single car on the northbound side of the bridge past the accident. Traffic on the southbound side just over a span of water crawled as drivers became onlookers. The tractor-trailer blocked traffic in the right lane and the wrong-facing car and the upside-down car blocked the left lane.

My father slid down to sit beside the woman. He called me to him, "Son, c'mere a second." I stumbled a bit but tried hard to disguise my pain and weakness. I was standing in front of my father and the woman, her blood now on his shirt.

"There's a kit in the back of my truck in that box. Also, beside those bags is a pack of water bottles. Get a couple of those waters and bring them over, would ya? I just wanna stop this bleeding till the medics get here." I nodded and turned toward my task in obedience, "Be careful. Don't hurt yourself any worse," ordered my father.

I returned to the back of his truck in pain and fatigue. A woman on a bike rode along the shoulder on the bridge. Silly place to ride a bike, I thought. I opened the back of the truck and found the water. I freed a couple of bottles from the packaging and set them down. I rummaged a bit through the storage bin in the back of his truck with my one left arm. I eventually found the kit. I closed the bin and set the water down on the bumper while I closed the truck topper. As I turned to return to the truck, I saw a couple of young men sitting in a car. One of them was outside the car, a red-headed young man standing with a drone.

The driver, a blonde boy who looked like a surfer, got out and came around to stand beside the boy with the drone. They were pointing at the accident scene. The drone was up. I never owned one or even wanted to, but it was fascinating to watch them control it. I surmised there was a camera on it and noticed that the surfer was alternating his view from the drone and the console the other red head was intently focused on. The drone passed the car in front of my father's truck and then shot right in front of the SUV as the biker flashed by in my peripheral vision.

My stomach churned and I jumped to the right side of dad's truck just in time to see the drone shoot in front of the biker. She screamed and ducked, losing control of the bike. I ran to her seeing her fall just as she was about to pass the space of missing barricade. This was the moment I was hoping not to see...my death. I would not run from it or close my eyes to watch it pass by me.

The woman screamed and grasped for the edge of the road as she slipped off it. I dove with both my arms outstretched. As she began her fatal fall to the alligator-infested waters below, I caught her wrist in my right hand.

Time slowed to a crawl, and it was as if I could see everything in front of me clearly. As the cyclist went fully over the edge, I willed my hand to ignore the pain my shoulder was about to draw attention to. Today wasn't the first time my shoulder was dislocated. It was a miserable pain, but I had been able to carry on with it. I needed to do that just once more before I died.

Her momentum pulled me with her. As I slid off the edge of the road, my left foot and left hand failed to grasp anything useful. Falling to our deaths in slow motion, was a thing I would not accept; her death or mine...not yet.

As I slid past the point of holding us on the road, I saw a metal tie rod from the destroyed barricade pointing toward the water below. It once held the concrete barrier in place, now it was my last chance to live; the cyclist's last chance to live.

The tie rod had a mass of concrete on the end of it and my hand burned in a sudden fire sliding down to it. It served as a hilt to keep my hand from sliding off the rod dropping me and the woman down into the water far below. My left hand knew how important it was to ignore the fiery sensation and just hold on.

My right shoulder felt like it was being torn free, but my right hand honored the earlier agreement. My left hand was holding fast to the iron rod, the one thing keeping us from falling to a very likely death. And so I hung there about a foot below the road, dangling in excruciating pain, holding onto the rod in my left hand and the cyclist dangling beneath me from my right hand. Her life was in my hand and mine depended on the strength of one hand and a single, rusted and bent, iron rod. I wanted to call out for help.

"Don't let me fall!" the cyclist screamed.

"HELP!" I tried to scream but couldn't get my lungs full of enough air to be very loud.

"HEEEELP USSSSS" the woman screamed.

The drone hovered above us uselessly. The way I took hold of the iron rod ended with my back facing the road. I looked up to my left and saw the young blonde man pointing feverishly down to the cyclist and me.

Time was no longer slow; not in the sense that I was calmly deciding what the next action was. Now, I was just dangling high above my death holding a frantic woman by the wrist as much of my body just wanted to let go of the bent rod that was continuing to bend slowly.

"HELLPP USSSSS!" the cyclist screamed again.

I could not get enough air to to do much more than breath through gritted teeth. But I struggled with nearly my last to get a prayer through my teeth.

"God... help me.... Save this woman.... before I die!" I begged. I tried to pull us up from my right arm. I forced a deep breath to give my body oxygen for the effort. It was too much. She was too heavy, and my ribs would not cooperate. I could not advance. If help did not come very soon, I would fail. I grunted as I tried again. I sounded more like I was being tortured rather than executing any sort of herculean effort.

My father's voice called down to me, "SON!"

I looked up to him. I could see the fear and panic in his face. He put his left hand on the iron rod holding us up and it bent farther down, threatening to come loose from the concrete it was mounted in.

"SAVE ME!!" she screamed. "I DON'T WANNA DIE!" she pleaded.

The seconds mounted up like heavy weights upon my joints and fire in my muscles. My grip was made strong over the years of turning small tight things in tiny places. Often, when others would need a wrench, I simply used my fingers. The years of using my hands served me now but even that would end soon.

"Dad...I forgive you," I strained to get the words out.
"WHAT?" he asked
"I forgive you, Dad," I repeated.
"Johnny, don't you give up on me. You never gave up on anything in your life. You better not stop now. You fight, you hear me. I'm coming and you BETTER FIGHT. I'm coming down there and if you don't want me to go in that water, you better not either. I'm coming."

One of the paramedics peered over the edge now along with the man I guessed to be the truck driver. The men formed a chain with my father's massive hands around my left wrist. He pulled, they pulled. I heard my father groan as he used all his strength to lift us. He was held by the trucker. The paramedic now grabbed my belt and pulled until I was high enough for him to reach the woman.

"I got her. I got her" he said.
But I would not let her go. My father, the trucker, and the paramedic, now aided by a police officer, pulled us up onto the road. No one let go of anyone.
I lay now on my father's chest, him clutching me. "MY SON!" he sobbed. "MY SON!"

The woman lay on the road looking at me, wiping her eyes, unsuccessfully. My father finally let me go and helped me to stand.

The woman stood. She hugged me now, "Thank you...for...for saving my life." The drone buzzed behind me.

"GET THAT SHIT ...OUTTA HERE!" the woman demanded. She turned to the young man controlling the drone. "YOU ALMOST KILLED ME! YOU SON OF A BITCH!" Now she was standing in front of the boy pointing in his face. I couldn't make out anything further that she said but she continued; she was waving her finger at the boy, then at the drone.

The paramedic took a long look at me, "You ought to come to the truck. C'mon." I just wanted to lay back down on the pavement. I felt beyond spent.

"That...was an amazing thing you did, son." My father grabbed me around my waist, pulling himself under my left shoulder to support me. He walked me to the ambulance where the woman was being treated.

"What happened to you?" she asked.

I smiled faintly through my exhaustion, "Just trying to get to church."

She nodded and lay her head back down on the stretcher. "What church?" she asked.

My father interrupted excitedly, "St. Luke's...on Underhill near the college." He rubbed my hair like I was just coming off the soccer field during a youth soccer match. "There's a service tonight...I guess we'll be starting a bit late, though."

"If I can make it, I'll be there...me and my daughter," the woman proclaimed. She had a bandage wrapped around her head, blood on her shirt. Other than that, she just looked like she'd had a long day. "I guess I'll have to find a ride though."

I had a feeling how the conversation was going to end so I listened to see what happened next.

"Actually, you probably need the rest...and you need to get checked out at the hospital," Dad suggested to her.

The woman swung her feet off the side of the stretcher, "I'm fine. I'll find a ride to that church tonight," she exclaimed.

The paramedic gave her an admonishing look, "Sit. Lemme finish."

My father looked at me. I smiled seeing that my silent prediction was correct.

"We have room...if you don't mind the back seat of a truck. There might be some food left over at the church. I can call ahead and have a plate saved for you," my father suggested.

It was as though I had seen all this unfolding before but perhaps it just made sense for the woman to want to go to church just as it made sense for me.

My father looked over to the cyclist, "My truck seats six!"

The woman chuckled, "Why not. I suppose I better say thank you to God, too."

Dad was even more excited now, "Outstanding. I can just put your bike on the back of the truck and drop you home later."

My father looked over to the boys, "Boys...why don't you follow me to church. I just have a stop to make."

They looked at each other. One of them responded, "We got valuable footage, man. Sorry."

I heard what the boy said about footage, but I really didn't care and so I gave it no further thought. I turned to go back to the truck.

"Hey buddy, let me take a look at you!" the Paramedic called out to me.

"Be right back," I said.

I walked to the back of the truck. It was not an easy walk. I put my right arm back into the sling with much effort and much pain. My legs now began to feel unstable, but they got me to the back of dad's truck. I sat down on the bumper, looking down at the two water bottles I previously came here to get. I was about to open one for myself and then the moment caught up with me. All that had just happened rushed to my thoughts at once and I felt the churn in my stomach.

My wobbly legs lurched into action and carried me to the barrier wall just in time to feel all that Texas hash and the French toast and asparagus and everything else still in my stomach suddenly come up. To throw up with cracked ribs...is a lasting pain.

I gathered myself and looked up, "You satisfied. Is there more?" I said to the skies. I struggled but made it to the back of the truck again. I drank one of the bottles of water. I took the other one in hand. The medi-kit was on the ground now. It seemed miles away. I tried to get down on one knee to get it, but everything hurt.

A woman who was watching me got out of her car. She ran to me, "I got it." She knelt down in front of me, picked up the kit, and extended it to me.

"Put it there," I nodded my head in the direction of the bin in the back of the truck. The top door was still open. She did as I asked. I took a few short breaths and gave the woman a smile of appreciation.

I took the water bottle into my hand and worked my way back to the ambulance where the woman was now standing. The paramedics were apparently done with her. Now, two of them were coming toward me, followed by my father. I met them about five yards from the paramedic's truck where the woman was standing. One of them slid himself under my left shoulder to support me. I got to their truck and I extended the water bottle to the woman, "For you," I said.

She smiled, shaking her head. The bottle was bloody. "Sorry about that," I said.

The paramedic took the bottle from her. "Give me that. We'll get you a clean one...that's cold," he said. He nodded towards one of the other paramedics who went inside the back of the truck. "Get two," he said. They pulled the bed on wheels beside me and lowered it. "Sit down buddy," the medic ordered. "Let's take a look at you."

They sprayed some treatment on my left hand and wrapped it. My outer shirt was torn, ripped down the front. The paramedic opened my outer shirt revealing my hero t-shirt.

"You picked a good shirt for today, dude," he said chuckling to himself.

My father was on his cell phone talking. I could hear bits of what he was saying, enough to understand that he was changing the format for church tonight.

He came to stand beside me, "Church is gonna start late tonight. I'll take you back to the house…"

I cut him off. "I'm going to church, dad – with you." I looked at him eye to eye. He was silent for a moment, recognizing my determination.

He nodded, "Okay." He returned to the phone, giving more instructions.

The paramedics finished with me. The tractor-trailer was now pulling into the left lane ahead. My father came to help me back to his truck.

"I got it," I said. "I'm fine, Dad." He nodded but walked slowly beside me.

I got into the truck with much effort. The woman with the upside-down car and her daughter were in the back seat. The cyclist I had saved was also in the back seat. They all smiled at me.

My father slid into the car victoriously. "You situated with your car?" he asked the woman sitting behind him.

"Oh, yes. It's going to be towed. The police gave me the name of the towing company. From there, I just have to give the insurance company the name of the tow company. I'm sure I'll get a rental in the morning," she explained.

"Well, ok," my father said, still seeming to feel excited. I studied him curiously. He caught my look, "What? Can't you tell when God is up to something incredible?"

That was almost funny. I was glad it wasn't because I did not want to laugh. "Where were you going anyway, dad? This isn't the way to your church."

"Oh, I just needed to take these water bottles and some t-shirts to a woman who is will be putting some screen prints on them for our church anniversary coming up. I'm paying her in water bottles for her son's soccer game this weekend. It'll be twenty-five years in a couple of months." My father was absolutely beaming.

"Oh...tonight will be a special service...I just know it. I don't know what God is up to, but I can't WAIT to see it!"

I agreed with my father but more than anything I wanted to go back to sleep. So, I leaned my head back as my father weaved through the emergency vehicles and headed up the empty road. I felt at peace now. I felt like maybe God was satisfied. Maybe he would let me live beyond today. Maybe I had earned that.

*I hope that's it, God. I don't know if I got any more in the tank now*, I thought.

"So, what was your name?" the cyclist asked me. "I...I mean, what are both your names."

"I'm Robert, Robert Boxton. That's my son Johnny," my father answered.

"What do you do, Johnny?" she asked. I just wanted to be left alone to sleep, but I did not want to be rude. "Car mechanic, body shop guy," I answered dryly. "Hey, ah, can I maybe...just sleep a bit? It's been a long day," I asked.

"Ahhh...sure...ahh...sorry," the cyclist apologized.

I'd made the cyclist uncomfortable. I didn't want to, but I also didn't want to talk even more. I just wanted to sleep. I hoped God was satisfied enough not to take my life now. I wanted to live too.

# My Last Name

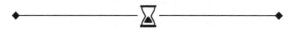

M y father pulled into the parking lot of his church. I hadn't seen it in a long while. There was a huge white building annexed to it now. The parking lot used to be grassy with concrete wheel stops and unofficial understandings of where cars should and shouldn't park. Now it was paved and had trees. He passed the new building and parked in a spot that now had a sign indicating it was reserved for the pastor.

As he pulled in, a young man with a brightly colored vest walked up speaking into a walkie-talkie. Before the young man reached the truck, a set of double doors to the building opened and an older couple came out. I wasn't sure what Dad said on the phone before he got back into the truck on the bridge or what he may have said while I was asleep, but people were prepared for something.

The couple coming out had blankets to give care to the women in the back seat of my dad's truck. Three more adults came out and two young girls as well. It began to feel like the truck was swarming with people wanting to help. I didn't care much for it. I just wanted to go inside and hear my father preach a sermon and to see if God had any more miracles to explain this extraordinary day I was having.

One of the women coming out of the church wore hospital garb. I predicted she would want to take her own look at the women from the bridge and possibly me as well. She started with me, "Hey, Johnny...I'm SO glad to see you back. Let me just..."

I cut her off. "I'm fine. Have a look at the ladies," I instructed.

"Baby, you don't LOOK fine! I'm gonna just..."

I looked sternly at her. "I'm fine," I said not blinking, feeling a deep sense of irritation.

I struggled to get out of the truck. I demanded that my mouth not proclaim my pain even if my facial expressions could not, would not withhold the secret.

"Hmmph...you look like you need to be in the hospital instead of arguing with me...suit yourself." The woman left me alone to look after the woman from the car.

The cyclist came to stand beside me, "Please, let me help you. It's the least I can do."

I was even more annoyed, but she asked me precisely in the way she had to for me to relent. "I'm fine...but ok," I said.

"I know...I know...you're fine. Just indulge me. Please. And, thank you," she said playing politics with my emotions.

We all made it to the building. The cyclist and I stepped inside.

"Welcome to our fellowship hall!" my father proclaimed to us as we all followed him inside. Some people came to lead me to a table near the area I guessed to be the front. There were some men I thought I recognized. They all seemed to recognize me.

"Make yourselves comfortable. We'll be serving a bit of dinner and then we'll have services. I gotta run to the back for a second," my father explained as he trotted away.

An older gentleman addressed me, "Hello, Johnny. You probably don't remember me. I taught shop class at high school." I studied his face and I suddenly recognized him through his beard.

"Mr. Fields?" I asked.

He nodded. "That's right. We heard that you and your father were heroes today...you especially."

I didn't know how to respond. "Maybe," was all I could muster.

My father came out of the back where I guessed the food was. "Everyone, please...let me have your attention." My father's voice boomed but someone handed him a microphone anyway. He took the mic graciously. "Can...can you hear me?"

His voice boomed across the room from the speakers in various places in the ceiling and on the walls. A woman cried out, "LOUD AND CLEAR."

My father chuckled and lowered the mic away from his mouth a bit. "Friends and family, thank you...thank you all so much for staying late for services tonight. I'll say grace and we can eat. If you don't mind, I'll give you a little time to eat and then I'm gonna jump right into the sermon for tonight."

A large screen up on the wall showing different images reenacting biblical scenes related to food and eating. One picture showed Jesus standing before a basket overflowing with fish. Another was of the twelve disciples passing bread and a cup. Another showed a young man touching a water barrel and another had a woman washing his feet.

I looked around the room and saw a few familiar faces. There was the boy from the diner this morning. Elliot was there. My father asked that we all bow our heads, which we all did.

"Father God in heaven and here on earth, we thank you – we thank you for your grace and your mercy. We thank you, Father God, for Silvia and her daughter Jamie and that you kept them from serious harm in the car accident. We thank you, Oh God, for the life of Annessa who you touched my son to save. We thank you, Oh Lord for touching my son today to accomplish what he did today. We thank you for this great assembly of workers in Christ who have come to share their hearts for one another and learn of your word and your works today Lord. We pray you continue to awe us, enthrall us, and convict us with your spirit and your care, Oh God. And now, Lord, we ask that you bless this food we are about to receive. We give thanks to the hands of your love shown through the hands that prepared it. We ask that it be nourishment for our bodies as you nourish our spirits Lord for the work that lay ahead in your service. We ask it all in the precious name of thy son, Jesus Christ."

The entire room joined in saying Amen.

After my father asked God to bless the food, some people began forming a line. I was a little hungry but more than anything I didn't want to stand in a long line. I didn't want to stand holding a plate in one hand and a drink or utensils or whatever, in the other hand. I was sore everywhere, even in places that weren't injured. I think I was mentally exhausted as well.

Those who didn't get into the food line, it seemed, were making their way to me. It was Lilliard first, closely followed by Elliot and the boy from the diner and then Ricky. The woman and her child were standing in the line. The cyclist came out of the far side door and reached me about the same time as the small crowd.

Elliot spoke first, "So...we've been...ahhh...comparing notes, I guess you'd say. I overheard Lilliard talking to somebody about you and I chimed in. Then that kid joined the conversation – you know how that goes." I nodded.

The cyclist interrupted, "Let me get you something to eat first." I nodded towards her. She listed the things they had in the back.

"Chicken is fine. Get me double mac and cheese. If they have cold cokes, I want two of them," I explained.

"Absolutely," beamed the cyclist. She had a funny walk and watching her move with the tight-fitting biker's shorts with the padding in the back was strange to me. I guess I just didn't understand biking.

Lilliard continued where Elliot left off, "So, uncle...you have been out saving people all day long, huh?"

"I guess," was all I said. They sat next to me or across from me. "Save a seat for that bike lady ...since she's getting my food," I requested.

The young man from Debbie's diner was there. I remembered his name; Dale. He was with a young lady and he was holding a baby.

"Mister," he said. "I called this church today. I talked to the pastor...your father." He paused, obviously full of emotion. "I brought my family. I'm glad they could meet you." He began to stumble over his words. "I called that shop too. Mr. Jimbo said...." His eyes welled up. "He said if you told him I'd get a job, then I have the job." He struggled to restrain his emotions. "I love cars, Sir. He said I can start work tomorrow." He gathered himself. "He said, whatever you're into, he hopes you're ok."

Lilliard tapped me on the shoulder, "Unc."
I looked up. He motioned his head to the right. I looked to see Julie standing in front of the right-side door to the kitchen was Julie. She was wearing plastic gloves and a white apron. Her hair was longer than I remembered, and she seemed a bit thinner. She wasn't wearing make-up and she was beautiful. She clutched her hands to her chest. She started blinking as though her eyes were filling with water.

I stood, painfully, from my seat. My legs seemed to have had their fill of compensating for my back and my ribs. I tasked them to stand once more anyway.

Julie seemed a bit in shock, but she started walking towards me. Then my legs carried me towards her. Her pace quickened and then she was wrapped around me. Her hair filled my nostrils. It was the sweetest smell. It filled a place in my soul that had been empty for a long time. To hold her was a singular joy that I tried to pretend I could do without. At this moment, I remembered how much I longed to hold her. Before the tragedy, she was what I dreamed of. I would wake in the middle of the night and see her lying beside me, and I would quietly thank God for my dream being true.

Making her happy, seeing her smile....at me...had been the thing I wanted most in all the world. After we lost the baby...after trying so hard to have one...that had all been taken away. It became too much to bear. But now I didn't care. My dream was true again...at least at this moment.

"You came, I prayed you would come...for so long," she said crying softly.

"I didn't know you'd be here," I said. "But I'm glad you are." I paused. "I'm not sure how much time I have, but...I want to apologize." Julie was now looking into my eyes.

"Apologize? For what?"

118

I looked down at her neck, away from her eyes. "I...I couldn't stand that look in your eyes. The...the smile...in your eyes...was gone after...." I couldn't say the words. "I...it hurt too much to see your eyes like that. I didn't handle it well."

"Oh, Johnny. I'm the one who's sorry. I knew how much you might be hurting... but...I'm sorry Johnny. I'm sorry I...pushed you away."

I reached into my back pocket. I held up the divorce papers. "I signed these. Do you still...."

Julie took them from me and opened them. She looked at me, "Johnny...I never really...I just wanted you to be like you were ...before..." She started to tear up the papers.

I stopped her. "You sure ...you sure you want me back? I figured...." It was hard to say what I was thinking. I figured you probably moved on...to some other guy by now." I closed my eyes and took a breath. "You're so beautiful..."

She stopped me. "No other man matters...except for Jesus Christ, Johnny. There's never been anyone else but you."

She kissed me and the world faded away. I opened my eyes and looked into hers. Her eyes smiled again...at me.

I put my forehead to hers, "Please God, let me live," I mumbled.

"What? What did you say, Johnny?" Julie asked.

I looked away from her eyes not sure how to respond.

She lifted my chin, "Look at me. What happened to you? What are you talking about?" she said waiting for my answer.

"Jules...can we just be at church tonight? I'll talk to you about it after."

Her eyes searched back and forth for a measured response. "Do you remember the first time we met?" I asked. "It was on the soccer field at that YMCA you used to go to. We were short on teams to compete against and our team traveled to your YMCA. Your nephew, Lilliard was coming off the field. He took a shot and the other team's goalie made an amazing stop... and our whole sideline was moaning. I was giving one of his teammates some instructions and you were walking up. You were the only one clapping. I stopped to watch you. Lilliard ran up to you and you hugged him. He was so excited to see you as were his parents." I smiled, "It was my second time seeing you...first was at that youth conference and you were singing. I felt just like that again just now...seeing you standing there."

She studied my face, and I knew she was wondering where my story was going. I continued, "Then the teams were invited to go to the pool at the YMCA after the game. You swam some laps while the kids played in the water. You were graceful like a mermaid in the water. I could have watched you the whole day. Then after you swam you came over to say good-bye to Lilliard and his family. What did I ask you?"

She looked at me curiously, "You asked me if I went to church nearby."

"Yes, I did. You told me where and what did I say next?" I asked.

"You said, "God be willing I'll be at your church tomorrow morning." I nodded. I was about to say something I thought might be clever and she interrupted me.

"Johnny, what if I said I couldn't wait till tomorrow morning. You're my husband and I want you to come home tonight." She tore up the signed divorce papers and put them on the table. "Whatever is going on with you right now...I'm with you."

My whole spirit smiled. "Then I'll tell you all about it...tonight...at home." I moved a seat out for her. "Sit with me." The cyclist smiled at us, her hands to her chest, and sat to my left. "You used to make macaroni and cheese for me."

Julie sat down. "Taste it," she said.

It was warm and perfect. It was like a fresh memory of joy calling my taste buds to attention. I could not help but smile knowing the only person who could have made it. "You made this!"

Julie blushed a bit and her face lit up with pride at my recognition.

"It's as good as I remember," I said heaping more of it into my mouth. "Better...because I haven't had it in ages. You stopped making it long before you put me out," I continued, my mouth still full of it.

A young man ran up to my father who sat not far away, his plate sitting in front of him untouched. Dad had been watching me, taking in all the people thanking me and welcoming me and my being reunited with Julie. His face changed and he began pointing to the large screen feverishly and waving to someone.

He stood and someone handed him a microphone. He walked to an open area in the room, "Everyone! Let me have your attention, please. It seems that today's amazing events were captured on film and they have been talking about it on the news."

My father looked over at the young man who was doing something with some wires coming out of the wall to the right of the kitchen door. The young man held up his thumb and the screen flickered from scenes of Jesus and food to a blank screen and then it flickered again to a newscast. The volume was loud. Dad gave instructions for the volume to be reduced and then all eyes were on the screen.

A television commercial was ending, and a local newscaster started explaining some upcoming footage.

*Welcome back. Earlier, we reported footage taken of a tragic accident. It might have been fatal had it not been for the acts of a man who risked his life to save another. We will share this amazing footage in just a moment, but we have even more reporting on this heroic lifesaver. But first, here's that footage.*

A smaller image appeared in the upper right of the screen next to the woman on explaining this afternoon's event. It was the footage from the drone the boys on the bridge had. It showed me diving to save the woman and then hanging over the edge of the bridge, one hand on the iron bar and the other on her wrist.

I looked over at the cyclist sitting beside me. She looked at me with a look of gratitude. It was an eerie feeling watching myself hanging over the edge of the bridge.

The newscaster continued: *We reported this footage to you live earlier, but now we have additional information. The man, still unidentified, was also reported to have saved the life of ANOTHER young woman who just called in. She reported that her boyfriend tried to...throw her off a ROOF today...my goodness...and the same man saved her nearly being killed himself. Authorities are on the lookout for the boyfriend. We will get your more details on that as they are available.*

The newscaster stopped speaking for a moment. *But there's more folks. This same man was also apparently having breakfast this morning at a diner and stopped an attempted robbery there. The owner of the diner has just called in. She's refusing to give any information on the man. Apparently, the hero...well, let's just call him that, our local hero disarmed the robber and got him to sit down and talked to him. The owner of the diner reports that patrons there that morning overheard the conversation the hero and the would-be-robber had, and the suspect was given some advice on how to get medicine for his sick child and ....and a job...where to go to get a job. An amazing series of events folks. This is truly...*

The newscaster stopped again, touching her ear. *Folks, this may be hard to believe but we have another caller. This...this hero, he has apparently done other great deeds today. We've also located the man himself. We will have cameras on scene when we come back to try to interview our local good Samaritan. Only here at Channel 7 news folks. For now, we'll get you that weather update concerning some activity out in the gulf.*

The news switched to a different woman on-screen standing before an animated weather graphic.

"Can we turn that off...please?" I requested. I recalled that earlier this morning, I did say to myself that I wanted to be a hero. But right now, I just wanted to have church and then be lie down beside Julie. "It's...it's REALLY been...a long day. I was kinda looking forward to coming to church before the night was over."

Dad looked over to me as though he hadn't understood. I was hoping that God had decided to spare my life. It seemed like perhaps this was so. However, it felt like I was supposed to have just one more service in case my hopes were wrong. I was also annoyed that it sounded like the news was going to come and interrupt the service.

I stood, painfully, to speak. "Dad, can we turn that off and ...can you give us a service tonight?" I pleaded. Julie's hand was now tucked under my arm wrapped around my elbow in the sling.

My father conceded, waving his hand to the young man in the corner. The screen flickered and went back to the images of Jesus with people and food.

"Well...son...I am proud of you. Many of us here are." He looked around the room. "We are in God's house and so let's hear a word from the Lord." My father began a prayer to bless tonight's message.

After his prayer, he asked to have Philippians chapter one, verses one through eleven brought on screen.

*So if there is any encouragement in Christ, any comfort from love, any participation in the Spirit, any affection and sympathy, 2 complete my joy by being of the same mind, having the same love, being in full accord and of one mind. 3 Do nothing from selfish ambition or conceit, but in humility count others more significant than yourselves. 4 Let each of you look not only to his own interests, but also to the interests of others. 5 Have this mind among yourselves, which is yours in Christ Jesus,[a] 6 who, though he was in the form of God, did not count equality with God a thing to be grasped,[b] 7 but emptied himself, by taking the form of a servant,[c] being born in the likeness of men. 8 And being found in human form, he humbled himself by becoming obedient to the point of death, even death on a cross. 9 Therefore God has highly exalted him and bestowed on him the name that is above every name, 10 so that at the name of Jesus every knee should bow, in heaven and on earth and under the earth, 11 and every tongue confess that Jesus Christ is Lord, to the glory of God the Father.*

He set his bible down onto the podium. "I have read for you the New International Version." He addressed his aides to the side again, "Now, let's turn to Romans...Romans chapter five; verses six to eight. Let's all read that aloud this time. And we read,

*You see, at just the right time, when we were still powerless, Christ died for the ungodly. 7 Very rarely will anyone die for a righteous person, though for a good person someone might possibly dare to die. 8 But God demonstrates his own love for us in this: While we were still sinners, Christ died for us.*

Dad continued, "It's all amazing to me as well. This was a sermon I was led to prepare for on Monday morning during my prayers. In my spirit, I knew...I knew I needed to preach on personal sacrifice...laying it all out on the line for our brothers and sisters; not just in Christ but even those that do not profess Christ, haven't accepted Christ as their savior."

Dad rubbed his lips, shaking his head, "The world looks at us and they feel confused. They hear us say that we are to love our neighbors as ourselves, but we are caught up in as much ungodly, worldly stuff as those we SAYYYYY are lost! So, what does it look like? What does sacrificing yourself for others look like?"

Dad looked around the room. People looked at me. The cyclist began to shudder in tears. She tried to restrain it, but her shoulders would not lie. My father continued, "Certainly, my son...my son has made me VERY, VERY proud all of his life—especially today. What he did today, as wonderful as it was, it doesn't compare to what Christ did for us! For each of US! The life he lived in serving others, the pain he endured at the hands of the Roman soldiers...even before he was crucified...he suffered and endured ALL of this so that he would be a worthy sacrifice, acceptable to God ...for US!"

He let it sink in just a few seconds, scanning the crowd. Then he continued, "So, then what? Christ died for us, in humility but he faced his death boldly. So, then if Christ died that we might live, do you think he went through all that trouble for us to be afraid to stick our necks out? NO!"

He looked over to his helper, "Joe, bring up second Timothy; chapter one, verse seven." The screen faded out of the previous set of verses to bring up the new one. "Let's read together," dad said.

*For the Spirit God gave us does not make us timid, but gives us power, love, and self-discipline.* 2Timothy 1: 7, NIV.

We read that verse and dad gave Joe another one. It was brought up on the screen and we all read it aloud.

*I know what it is to be in need, and I know what it is to have plenty. I have learned the secret of being content in any and every situation, whether well fed or hungry, whether living in plenty or in want. 13 I can do all this through him who gives me strength.* Philippians 4: 12-13, NIV"

The doors of the hall opened. A few people came in followed by cameramen. My father paused for a moment and went to the back to speak with them. They whispered for a while and then my father spoke to all of us.

"Folks, Channel Seven news is here. They want to interview anyone who was helped by my son today. But, first, we'll finish the service. They need time to get set up. While they get set up, I'll finish up the discussion. If any of you feel uncomfortable, please feel free to leave. But I...I believe God is up to something here and I intend to see it through."

No one got up to leave. The cameras got setup as my father returned to the front and continued. Meanwhile, more people came into the room, onlookers perhaps.

It was eerie. My father was sort of aloof – cool. But they were here because of me. I looked at Julie. I was expecting a look of uncertainty. Instead, I only saw pride.

She crossed her legs and leaned toward me, putting her left hand behind me to rest on my right shoulder. She brushed my face with the back of her right hand, "Must have been a heck of a day!" She smiled an innocent smile, watching my eyes.

"You okay?"

I dropped my head, the warm, soft touch of her fingers was soothing. "I...I just wanna come home. I'm tired."

Julie kissed my forehead, "Okay, Babe. I'll take care of you."

I closed my eyes and a feeling of gratitude washed over me. I wanted to go home with her right now and just sleep beside her. Julie was the kind of woman that could swim laps in the pool forever and then come home to do hours of yard work. She wrapped Christmas presents for her nieces and nephews in October. She cooked amazing meals...even better than my mom used to. She cleaned with a deep passion and everything always shined and smelled perfect when she finished.

She could have a conversation with anyone about anything and always had the right words to keep the conversation from becoming about a complaint. Everything she did or said made things better. She looked amazing in whatever she wore but she didn't have any need to be celebrated. I loved the way her slender wrist fit neatly into the small of my hands. I loved that she waited for me to come back to her after she pushed me away, and after I decided I couldn't bear to see the love she had for me clouded by pain. Today the pain in her eyes was gone. It was in my body now. That was a trade I would take every time.

Dad went back to his podium that had been dragged to the front of the hall. He continued, "So, not only does the model of Christ say to us that we should live and sacrifice ourselves for one another, it says we should do it without fear and we also are encouraged that we can live a life of contentment because God gives us strength to do what we need to do. Let's do one more. Give me Psalm 112."

Joe brought up the next set of verses. "Let's just do verses one and two and then we'll skip down to seven and eight."

He read these verses himself, "Praise the Lord. Blessed are those who fear the Lord, who find great delight in his commands. Their children will be mighty in the land; the generation of the upright will be blessed. They will have no fear of bad news; Their hearts are steadfast, trusting in the Lord. Their hearts are secure, they will have no fear; in the end, they will look in triumph on their foes.

"This was Psalm 112, one and two and seven and eight, NIV," dad explained. "So, we don't have to have fear. We can live without fear, God's people. When bad news comes...and it will...we can face it without fear. This is what the spirit of God allows us to do. My son, perhaps, was a present-day, watered-down version of what Christ did. But just think of it... just THINK of what we can accomplish for each other when we put aside all this fear and just live...just live like Christ's example. You are free to be the best YOU that you can be...Just LIVE and LOVE."

I felt washed in emotions. I felt like some of what I had seen and felt made sense but, in a way I didn't understand. It was more like...I think – I accepted all that had happened. I didn't actually need it to make sense and I felt an utterly indescribable connection to God suddenly. I felt lost in my own emotions. I felt like I was going to start crying so I held my tears as hard as I could.

I heard my father say, "Won't you give your life to Christ...let him show you how to live without fear, through His word, through his spirit, and through our fellowship."

My legs responded. Without meaning to, I stood. I felt washed in emotion overwhelmed with gratitude and love. I felt loved by my father. I felt loved by Julie. I felt loved by the cyclist. I felt loved by nearly everyone in the room. The room felt like waves of love hitting me over and over again. I was being carried by the waves and I became dizzy but not sick. My ribs hurt but I could breathe easier. My shoulder hurt but it didn't stop my hands from reaching to the ceiling.

My heart cried out in my chest to God. I had run from the call to serve God for years. After my mother died and my father's shame was revealed to me, how he'd been unfaithful to my mother while she was dying, that he'd found consolation outside our home, I resented my own desire to serve God.

At this moment, all of that was gone. All of the frustration I felt, all the bitterness I'd carried for the way my life had turned out was gone. Today, I had only gratitude in my heart. My lips spoke with words I didn't intend to use. I heard them say, "I'm here, Lord. I'm here."

Tears were flowing down my face, but it was more than tears. I was soaking wet. I looked up at the podium and the cross on the front of it. I knew now that God never intended to end my life physically. Today was the day that I was to unshackle myself from all my fear, all my jealousy and anger, and my regrets.

I realized I was on my knees. My shirt was soaking wet. My hair was soaking wet. My jeans were soaking wet. I was kneeling in a puddle of water. My pains were present still, but I was able to ignore them. I leaned forward, squeezing water out of my hair and then I wiped my face.

I looked around the room and it was silent. It was a room full of people staring, mouths open. A few people had cell phones out, presumably recording what they saw. The people in the back with the cameras were recording. Those not with the camera were simply staring.

I stood up, still soaking wet, my shirt clinging to me uncomfortably. I pressed my hair down to my scalp and pulled my hand down my face to wring my hair out. Then I wiped the water from my face. I looked up to my father and tears were flowing down his face. His fingers were interlaced with his hands to his mouth. He was speechless.

I scanned the room to find Julie. Her face was full of tears and her hands covered her mouth. She ran to me as I stood still in the puddle of water. The crowd of people in the room all seemed to come closer to me.

"Are you okay?" Julie asked me.

I was sore still but not like before, "I ...I feel good," was all the words I had. I could not describe the feeling I had. I felt...emptied. It was like all the baggage I'd been carrying emotionally all these years and had suddenly tried to let go of all day today was simply taken away. I felt free.

"What happened?" I asked Julie.

"I...I dunno. One minute you were standing next to me babbling something then you just walked to the podium and fell down on your knees. I blinked and you were wet...like really, really wet."

The crowd came in closer. People were touching my clothes, I guess to see if I was really wet. The next fifteen minutes were very strange. People were touching and squeezing my clothes to make water come out. People were crying. I heard the word "miracle" sooo many times. I think the real miracle was this whole day.

The news people tried to interview me to which I declined. People I had helped that day who were in the crowd started lining up to talk to the reporters giving statements. The crowd was loud, and I tried to work my way out of it pulling Julie behind me.

My father seemed to understand. He commanded folks, one by one, to let me out of the building and to give me space. I finally made my way outside with Julie still holding my hand.

He politely pushed a couple of people back into the hall and closed the door as nicely as he could. He was insisting that he'd be right back.

My father turned to me, "Well son, I'm so proud of you and happy for you. You know what you have to do now, right?"

I felt no more resentment to God now or to my father. "Yeah, dad." I nodded. "...and I'm ready...just not tonight. Tonight, I'm going home with my wife."

"Ahh, before you go, I just wanna..." he took the box out of his pocket with the ring he offered me earlier.

"You coming back to me?"

I took the box. "Yeah, Dad. I am."

His eyes watered and he nodded his head restraining a smile. I looked into Julie's eyes.

She smiled back and me and kissed me. "Goodnight, Dad!" Julie said to my father as we began to walk off.

I stopped to say one more thing. "I love you, Dad. I'll call you in the morning...we'll pick up my training where we left off... some years ago."

"I'd like that. I'd like that very much, Son." My dad turned to open the door and the voices from inside spilled out of the room until my father closed the door behind him.

"Did you drive?" I asked.

Julie smiled, "Yes. You probably shouldn't drive anyway."

I put my arms around her waist.

"YOU'RE STILL WET!" she shrieked pulling away from me laughing. "I don't think I'll ever get my mind around what just happened."

I sighed deeply, "It was one heck of a day. I'll tell you all about it...later."

"So, you're back to preaching tomorrow?" Julie asked.

I looked down at my pants. I pulled out a business card from earlier today, holding it up in the light from the building floodlights behind us. "Well, I think I gotta crawl before I walk and walk before I run. Besides, I think I gotta have some income to support my wife!"

"That would be great!" Julie said. "But tonight...you're mine Mr. Boxton."

"I'm all yours...Mrs. Boxton!" I said.

# Messenger

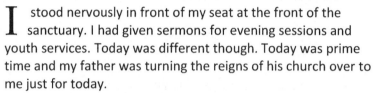

I stood nervously in front of my seat at the front of the sanctuary. I had given sermons for evening sessions and youth services. Today was different though. Today was prime time and my father was turning the reigns of his church over to me just for today.

My father stood at the podium introducing me, "My friends, my son has been preparing for this day for two years now. It has been two years nearly to this very day that he recommitted his life to the Lord...after a MOST interesting day. Today, from his preparation and God willing, with the Lord's spirit, my son will deliver a word from the Lord. It gives me great joy and pride today to sit and to watch the Lord work through my son."

I replaced my father's position standing at the podium. The crowd was huge. Annessa, the cyclist, was there. Silvia was there with her daughter. Elliot was there. My cousin Duck was playing the guitar softly. The woman that was taking care of Dooley before he died was there. The crowd was full of old friends and newer friends. But most importantly, my wife Julie was there. I smiled at her before I began. Julie was holding my twin sons of about three months old. I gripped the podium with both hands.

"Thank you, Dad...and my thanks to all of you for your support and for filling this house today." I bowed my head to pray, "God have mercy on me your servant. I pray Lord that these, your people, would not hear me but would hear you, that they would see not me but you, that their spirits would be emptied by my words and filled with your spirit and that their minds would be made ready to do your will. In Jesus' name, I ask for your presence and your power."

My nerves eased and I saw the crowd again. I felt love...it felt like peace coming to me in gentle waves. The sermon I prepared was one that I believe I was getting ready to preach for a long time now. And so, it began.

"My friends, turn with me, in your bibles to Psalm sixty-six, verse five. I want to talk to you today about The Process. When you think of the word, Process, you think of a series or sequence of events that all fold and work together to accomplish a goal. In fact, one of the definitions from Dictionary.com suggests that a process refers to a continuous action or a series of changes taking place in a definite manner."

The audio-visual team brought up the verses on the large screen.

"And it reads, 'Come and see what God has done, his awesome deeds for mankind!'"

I looked around the crowd and all eyes were fixed, waiting for me to continue and explain further. So, I continued, "Many of you remembered me kneeling in the fellowship hall nearly two years ago in a miraculous puddle of water. What I never told many of you is that it was not the first miraculous puddle of water I saw that day. I started that day waking from a dream that I was drowning only to find myself in a mysterious puddle of water on my mattress that never got absorbed into the mattress that morning.

But I'm not standing before you to talk about miracles or water puddles or dreams. I am here today, to talk to you about God's process. God's process to do what, though? I believe that God wants to resurrect you into a new life. That is what baptism is about. That morning, two years ago, my dream of myself drowning was accompanied by a word to my spirit...I knew I was going to die that day. What I did not know at the time is that it wasn't a physical death I was going to experience.

Glory to God that he didn't give me specifics that morning or that day would have gone very differently. The Lord only impressed upon my heart what I needed to know. So, maybe He's doing that with you right now...only giving you just enough info for you to change your direction with what you already know and feel.

So that day, I searched my feelings. Then, I went about righting wrongs and shedding myself of weights and encumbrances and freeing my mind of regrets and forgiving myself for my own faults. You see, I needed to do all the things I did that day in order to get myself ready for God's service.

But even more than that, I needed all those years preceding that moment...the years of anguish, the years of pain, the years of self-pity and doubt for that day to have meaning and for me to have been healed emotionally and then for me to stand before you today.

It was God's process. I could not be resurrected until I was first crucified. Oh, I wasn't crucified like Christ was – nails in my hands and feet. I was beaten that day by a few men, but I wasn't beaten like Christ was beaten—his back shredded by the Roman scourge–that whip they used to rip skin and muscle off the ribs in your back. I was accused that day of things I hadn't done and suffered for it just like Christ. But I didn't have to stand trial before the most powerful men in the land. At the end of that fateful day which marked the end of a fateful many dark years, I was resurrected.

In Psalm twenty-three, we see the story of David enduring great hardship. He said, Yes...I walk through the valley of the shadow of death BUT... I will fear no evil.

God's people, God didn't show David a way around the trouble. He took David THROUGH the trouble. May God have mercy on you to show you a way around your troubles, but God bless those of you whom he takes THROUGH trouble. Know that people are watching you–I believe the longer you are under the weight of your trial, the greater your testimony, the greater the Glory for God, and the greater the number of people will be encouraged to see that you can survive...even thrive in your troubles.   This is real freedom - when your sense of security isn't tied to a husband or a wife or a job or a bank account or having things go your way. When you feel no dependence on things that can be taken away from you...this is freedom. God wants to get you to this place, but He knows it takes time.

But this is God's process. It is different for everyone - and, for every believer. I was under for a long time y'all...I may still be under but today I have a loving wife, two loving children, in the presence of a loving father and loving church family in the presence of a loving God. Today I feel no pain or fear. Tomorrow may be different, but I thank God for today.

I thank God for bringing me through my troubles and resurrecting me from my own crucifixion. The pain of losing my mother and grandparents at an early age in such a slow, troubling way, the pain of being estranged from my father for years, the pain of losing a son, the pain of a failed marriage, the pain of lost friendships that I ruined—I endured years of doing work that I loved for powerful men that I feared – men that might kill me for looking at them the wrong way.

A long time ago, one of my father's friends, a deacon at the church we attended so many years ago quoted Romans eight and twenty-eight to me. You all know how it goes...All things work for the good of them that Love the Lord and are called to His purpose...doesn't it go something like that?

Well, you try to tell that to someone who is in the middle of being crucified and it may not go over that well. I said to the Lord that day under my breath, what good can come of all this?

That's what I said. You know what happened? That day, the preacher preached from John one verse forty-six. I remember it clearly. Nathaniel said when he heard that Jesus was from Nazareth, Can anything good come from there?

So, evidently, Jesus was raised up in a troubling place. How can anything good come from a place of trouble? Well, I tell you today that Jesus came from a place of trouble and no greater man walked the earth. To the unbeliever, Phillip said, 'Come and see.' That's what the believer said to me that day, when I didn't really believe. I was raised as though I believed but I didn't truly believe. I asked that day so many years ago, what good can come of all this? Deacon Mills told me, 'Come on in, young man.' Come on in and listen to what God has to say to you today. Maybe you'll feel better. That's what he said, 'Come on in...come see.'

I went into church that day. After I heard the message about a man being introduced to Jesus and Jesus knowing that man before he came to him. Jesus told him, 'I know you. I know all about you.' He said to Nathaniel, 'You may be amazed but you haven't seen anything yet.'

And so, you know what I said? I said to God in the church that day...I said, 'What are you up to? What is your plan?'

In John chapter one, verse thirty-nine, John the Baptist's disciples left him to follow Jesus. They asked him, where are you living...I can imagine the conversation today being something like, "What's going on, man?"

What does Jesus say to them? He said... 'Come and see.'

The Lord didn't say, I'll be on the corner of Lincoln Avenue and forty-third street if you need me. He didn't say, what you're looking for is on aisle 15 on the right side by the spray bottles. In verse thirty-nine of chapter one the Lord said, 'Come and see.' God wants you to be involved in what he's doing. He gave you free will to choose; to choose to obey, to choose to submit, to choose to commit, to choose to study his word, to choose to do good to others, to choose to stand up to those who don't. He invites you to be a part of His process...He says, Come and see – Come and see what I'm up to, come be a part of it.

Today, like David and Philip, I invite you come and see. I have shared some of my testimony to you because I want you to know that God can AND will carry you, lead you, comfort you and encourage you on your way through this world's troubles.

It's in Psalm twenty-three if you need to be reminded every now and then. Everyone has a cross waiting for them but not everyone has accepted God's resurrection. For those of you not carrying a cross, just keep walking and waking up. For those who are in the middle of your troubles, I encourage you today that there is a way through. There is the possibility of a resurrection and I invite you to come and see."

The words fell from my lips. I realized that I'd stopped following my notes and just letting the words flow through me and so I just let it flow.

"I want to suggest to you that even though the bible reminds us that we have the freedom to choose and have had it so since Adam and Eve chose to disobey God in the garden... even though we have free will, God still has a plan. In order to help us and allow us to participate in HIS plan, he takes us through a process. We don't get ready to do something important all in one stroke, it takes...a Process.
    And so, as we read Psalm 66, verse 5 of the NIV version, it says...
    'Come and see the works of God; his awesome deeds for mankind.'
    In the early parts of the old testament, we see that God performed miracles and God's people still fell away. God healed, he sustained miraculously, he preserved his people in slavery, in lion's dens, in fiery pits, in all kinds of circumstances but still...God's people lost faith. They had to continually be reminded and be taught again.
    In Matthew, chapter twenty-eight, verse six. The angel of the Lord says, Come and see. Come and see that the Lord is risen. And we also see King David saying to those he ruled over in Psalm sixty-six verse five, come and see. David wants to take you through the history, David wants to impress the present upon you as well."

I felt really good. I noted that I felt so much peace allowing these words to flow through me as I continued.
    "You see God teaches us by showing us. He shows us IN OUR LIVES. We don't learn from the outside of the mystery. We

learn from the inside of the calamity. You need to come and see. But you need to also be shown. It cannot be given to us. It has to be shown to us - over time. It's not an event. It's a process. It's a lifestyle. It is a standard by which you live.

Come and See: it's a process of learning to see things differently. It must be experienced over time - day by day. We must embrace the process.

Come and see. It's a commitment. It's a choice. You have to leave where you are in order to get someplace new.

Come and See: it implies you have to be willing to open your eyes and your heart and see something new. He teaches us by showing us over time. Listen to his word, his mind, his heart. Draw closer. You see a little more as you draw closer to him. It's a process. To live by his power, by his influence, waiting on his blessing, following him, waiting for him.

He doesn't want you to drown but he does want you to swim. Because there are others drowning today. I don't know how strong a swimmer you are. But there are people drowning. The world is drowning.

But I know what you're thinking. I know how you feel. I know you want for God's plan to make sense to you. I know you want him to explain it all to you not just a little bit. What I have decided is that his plan is too complicated for us to really understand.

If a physicist came in here today and began explaining how the wind works and how the moon has an impact on the wind the weather and how the tilt of the sun at different times of the year created season you would probably tune him out. It's too much and all you really care about is whether it's going be raining when you get up to walk to the car. But, that's what the physicist was trying to explain all along...it's not going be raining and here's why. But you don't want to hear all that...is it going be raining or sunny...when I go outside. When I get home, I no longer care. I don't care about cloud cover and what weather systems are out on the Atlantic or in the Gulf of Mexico. I don't care about what month of the year it is and where the Earth is in its axial rotation and its revolution around the sun.

I have decided to just trust God. I trust that his plan is better than mine. I believe he can see wider and farther ahead than me. I believe God knows what I'm truly capable of because I believe he made me. I believe that God is gentle enough to show me only what I can handle as I grow and strengthen and become wiser.

I now want God to show me what he's up to...not because I don't believe he's up to anything at all like I used to feel...but because I want to get even closer to him. I'm excited to see what he does next. This is a part of my testimony. I will take the difficult things with the easy things...there is no good or bad...there's only what is and what is not."

The crowd was clapping fiercely, and people were standing. I felt my work was nearly done. I was satisfied with having allowed God to use me this morning. I closed my eyes, still taking in the love and peace before I continued,

"As I take my seat this morning, I invite you to let God lead you through your troubles. Let God help you to focus on your part in His plan instead of your frustration with the results of yours. Allow God to show you what he's up to, trust Him to give you little glimpses of what comes next and then have no fear. Let him prepare a table before you in the middle of your enemies. Let him pour your cup until it runs over. Let him anoint your head with oil. Let God EXALT and ELEVATE you AFTER he's taken you through your Valley of the shadow of death. When the Lord says, 'COME SEE' I urge you...to get up, get involved and participate in God's plan for your life and don't be afraid of trouble. Just keep your eyes on God...let him show you what comes next."

My hands spread wide into the air, and I continued. "God is asking you to COME and SEE what he has to show you. When he calls you, if you're carrying something heavy in your life, you gotta put it down, or put down what you're struggling with in your spirit to make room for him. You might have to leave some things behind in order to come and see. Is God calling you today to let go of some things and let him show you something new?"

I looked around, feeling charged with otherworldly energy, clutching the sides of the podium.

"My friends, my beloved, I encourage you to follow God humbly wherever He leads you – come. I implore you to wait for God patiently wherever he keeps you, let him show you – open your eyes and see. I challenge you to go boldly wherever God sends you – to show others. Thank you."

The remainder of the crowd stood, and the room erupted in clapping and cheering. I felt satisfied with the support but mostly I hoped that somewhere amongst the crowd, my words actually helped someone.

My father stood and took his place at the podium as the Senior Pastor of the church. My mind faded to a series of events leading up to today. I thought of all the things I counted as misery earlier. I forgave myself for my mistakes and I let go of all my burdens.

I sit here now feeling free—free from my burdens, and I only feel gratitude. I have my wife. I now have kids. After the old man died, I was deeded a successful car repair franchise worth $10 million in inventory and revenue. I have my father back in my life. I have been mentoring and working with young men here at my dad's church. I am free to give love in so many ways. The more love I give, the more love I get back.

I am grateful for the difficult things, the easy things, the hard things, and everything else. I have more in my heart to give than any need to receive….and this …this makes me free. I shook my head in utter amazement. This is what God has been saying all along - God is amazing.

# Epilogue

I thank you for taking the time to take this journey with Johnny. I wanted to illustrate some of the different kinds of weights that we carry that we need to fee ourselves of before we can be truly effective advocates of whatever message or efforts we hope to make our lives to be about.

As a bible-believing Christian, I hope that this work opens your mind towards embracing Christ. However, as an aspiring philosopher, I would count it progress if you are at least to embrace the depth of your own truth and shed the weight of so many shallow and pointless things we are drawn to in the American culture. In my learnings thus far, there is a good deal of overlap between some of the teachings of our great philosophers and those of Christianity.

Above all, I pray that you would seek peace, firstly with yourself, and secondly with all men and that you would strive to become your best self. I do not believe that the continual effort to attain and maintain peace equates to complacency. In fact, the notion of achieving inner peace strikes me as something that requires both sacrifice and experience. Peace is not the same as calm. Calm would be the absence of any sort of conflict, agitation or high energy. I define Peace as the willful and sustained presence of calm despite being in the midst of chaos or conflict or some high energy state.

I believe that truth, not your opinion or attitude toward any particular truth or your response to some truth, is a path to peace...peace that is not dependent on the existence or availability of a physical thing.

I pray your journey leads you through a life-altering and recognizable truth and that you have both the awareness of it and the will to choose it...over your comforts, if need be.

I would be ever so grateful for your support of my ministry to produce literature in the overlap between Christianity and the secular world with your Amazon review.

# About the Author

For additional works by Thelonius, please visit Amazon and search "japoc."

I was born in the small, yet growing, town of Lakeland, Florida, in the early seventies. As the younger of two children, I was the only son to an English teacher fully devoted to personal service at her Baptist church and a practical-minded, problem-solving Chemistry teacher. I became familiar with two distinctly different, complementary, and sometimes conflicting views on life. I graduated with honors from Alabama A&M University with a bachelor's degree in Mathematics and a minor in Computer Science. I then completed a Master's degree in Statistical Computing at the University of Central Florida.

I began writing poetry in high school and continued through college and my post-baccalaureate education and beyond. I am often called upon to write poetry for family events or local funerals. To construct my works, I draw from years of teaching Sunday school to shape my poetic works into rhythmic, uplifting prose. I also studied martial arts and tend to draw upon this experience to create vivid action scenes.

I am married to Angela Chestang, my college sweetheart, with whom I share a son and a daughter. My youngest child, who survived a dramatic lifesaving and life-altering brain surgery, continues to teach me to focus on what is most important and not to sweat the small stuff. Frequent hospital visits and a carefully crafted lifestyle centered around my daughter's health enables me to relate well to the complexities in the lives of others.

After years of successful work in technical support and technical support management, I experienced layoffs and used the time between jobs to embrace my identity as a writer. I also fell into the study of Philosophy; Stoicism, in particular. Despite having already published three books, I finally embraced writing as a profession in 2019.

I have chosen to use my ability to bring vivid imagery and colorful storytelling into the service of worship. My hopes are to write sobering, PG-13 Christianity for the young Christian mind or for those that have contemporary questions about why they should follow Christ. My goal is not to preach to Christians but to encourage non-Christians or those "straddling the fence" that there is a personal God who has a plan for each of our lives; one that we each must take an active part in.

I believe God is shaping and molding me into my best me as he does for all of us, if we allow Him – which makes me JAPOC; Just Another Piece of Clay (Isaiah 64:8).

Made in the USA
Coppell, TX
22 September 2020